PROMETHEUS II

By
S. J. BYRNE

ARMCHAIR FICTION
PO Box 4369, Medford, Oregon 97504

*For more information about Armchair Books and products, visit our
website at...*

www.armchairfiction.com

Or email us at...

armchairfiction@yahoo.com

GODS IN SPACE!

The warlords of Russia had made a strange alliance with the underworld— and now all the democratic peoples of Earth were about to pay the price for one man's arrogance. Humanity's only hope lay with the Gods in space…

Stephan Germain was not just an average journalist. He was gifted with the exceptional ability of really getting people to listen. And listen they did...even in the far outer reaches of the Universe.

Prepare yourself to join Germain and his trusted allies in this epic "Good vs. Evil" science fiction adventure where America and the free peoples of the world unite to fight against—Armageddon!

CAST OF CHARACTERS

STEPHAN GERMAIN
By luck of the genetic draw this man found himself deep in Russian held territory fighting for his life.

DOCTOR JULIUS BORG
This twisted scientist was as ugly as the unspoken atrocities that occurred in his secret hideaway.

NICHOLAS THE FIRST
The very personification of absolute power. Would his quest for world domination succeed?

PVT. SERGEYEV PAVLOVICH
This disgraced soldier was determined to bring in the man who'd brought him down.

LILLIAN GERMAIN
She'd left for the frontlines with one driving need—to get to her man before the Russians did.

MAJOR MICHAEL "SLIM" KENT
A soldier's soldier if ever there was one. His loyalty to friend and country would never be put to question!

THE DEROS
Malevolent underground creatures, believed to be no more than a child's fairy tale. But they were real—and they were deadly.

PROLOGUE

SOMEWHERE within the youngest mountains of the world is a man who sits on a magnificent throne, in a great palace in a great cavern. The cavern is a mile long, but it is only one small part of a vast chain of caverns, which in turn are connected by man-made tunnels to an incredible system of deep caverns which, if followed, could lead one even beneath the seas and to other continents—even to America. But these connecting tunnels are walled off and heavily guarded against a dread and ancient foe, against the cruel, detrimental forces of Hell, itself. And this place, which dares to resist and stand firm through the ages of time against the evils of the Pit, is a secret and wondrous place whose name is known to thousands of advanced mystics on the surface of the world. It is called—*Agarthi*. And the great man who sits on the throne is called the King of the World.

In fact, he could enforce his rule upon all the surface world, if he were confident that he could first conquer and control the jealous foes of Agarthi. This is all that holds him back. His conquest of the surface world would be a benevolent one, because his weapons could render us as helpless as white mice in a cage, and without killing a man, for those ancient weapons were fashioned, in unthinkable eons past, by the hands of wondrous beings whom the surface people, in their egotistical disdain of things they could not reduce to their own limited understanding, called the legendary "gods" of the heathens.

This King of the World is ages old, yet he looks as ever-young as Apollo. Although a great science is behind the reasons for his immortality, the surface folk would call it miraculous. In his cool, benevolent eyes is a power and fearlessness mingled with vast wisdom. If he were fully the

King of the World there would be no more of wars and fears and wasteful bungling.

Once every fifty years or so, this King of the World is accustomed to making an oracular statement to his people concerning the coming events for the next fifty years. The previous prophecy had been made before the turn of the century and had been noted by a certain Russian who was privileged to be present. This prophesy was brought to the surface world and published, but no one seemed to take it very seriously, until the events predicted began to happen with mathematical precision. He predicted World War I, he told what powers would be involved and what would be the consequences. He also predicted World War II.

On the night of August 14, 1945, however, he was moved to call his people together to prophesy again…

"This great surface-world war, which I have predicted," he said to them, "has not really ended. It has left too many things unsolved and unconquered. In twenty years the dragon seeds sown by this war will sprout overnight into full bloom, and it will be worse than ever. America itself will totter on the brink of disaster under the merciless blows of the most ruthless Dictator of all the present surface-world's written history. But the threat of this one man will not be the only shadow to darken the light of hope for surface men, for he will bring with him a horror so great and overwhelming that even he, himself, will seek to escape from it. He will seek to make a treaty with—*our most despised enemy.*"

The assembled elders of Agarthi and all the entranced people behind them gasped in horrified amazement. He raised his hands for silence. His great, deep eyes looked far into the corridors of time.

"Our enemy shall then be strong, and much more organized than he is now. Our foe will of course betray this stupid surface man, and he will threaten the world with what

Christians refer to as Armageddon. At a time when we of Agarthi are as yet unprepared, *they* will make ready to strike, and it will be a dark and tumultuous time for all the world—a black hour of hopelessness and despair…"

"But let us then prepare ourselves now to deter *them*, oh my King!" cried one of the elders, greatly troubled.

The King again gestured for silence. "There comes to my mind a sense of something which is incomprehensible to me. I seem to see a common variety of surface man who—in that hour—will help *us*, although I know not what thing a surface man could do to—" The prophet looked with a wondering expression as though into a world which lay within himself. "I sense a tremendous power, like that of one of the Elder Gods, and with this surface man I associate the ancient legend of Prometheus, for there are many points of similarity. But I know not what that power will be, nor whence it will come."

"What is this man's real name?" queried another of the elders.

"I know not, nor can I see his face, because he goes disguised to the work of world salvation. There is nothing more beyond this event, except that Agarthi will work *with* this man, and he will do a wondrous thing that is too stupendous for me to grasp."

"And what else is there?" asked another elder.

The King's eyes focused at last upon the assemblage before him. "That is all," he said.

And they knew him well enough to know that he would not prophesy again until the mysterious event predicted had come to pass…

CHAPTER ONE
The Dictator

"JUMPIN' catfish!" said the Quichua Indian.

He shaded his black, hawkish eyes and his high, brown cheekbones to inspect a whirring object that was marring the perfection of a clear Bolivian sky. By means of a dusty rope he halted the march of his bushy-haired burro, and watched intently as the sinister object drew closer. Then he turned suddenly and continued his way toward Santa Cruz. He sucked coca juice out of the sodden wad in his cheek and spat it purturbedly at the dirt, which apparently represented the land of his sadly duped ancestors.

"Get along, Fuzzy," he addressed the burro, in Yankee English. "But keep a straight face, will you? That Russian buzzard thinks we're dead meat, and unless your uncle does some fast thinking he may be right!"

His own face was as expressionless as stone, except for a flash of inextinguishable hatred and bitterness in his eyes. His pulse beat a little faster now to keep up with the rate of his thinking, because he knew with a certainty that somewhere within the next ten minutes he would either kill someone or be killed himself. As calmly as possible, he calculated the speed and angle of descent of the thing above and behind him and how soon his own painfully slow progress would bring him to the turn in the road ahead. There was a fairly high bluff there, topped by the incipient brush of the Bolivian *montania**. If he could just get around it in time to avoid getting shot before making a dash for cover!

---

* *Montania.* Typical low, scrubby jungle of the Bolivian *Oriente, Pando* and *Beni* regions—author.

SLOWLY and almost noiselessly, the shiny black rocket-gyro drifted on its whirling blades toward the two quaint figures on the road below. Twenty or thirty years before, the appearance of such a contraption over the hills of Cochabamba or the passes and jungles beyond would have caused considerable excitement among the sparsely distributed inhabitants, but in this year of 1970 everybody south of the La Paz-Asuncion line had become accustomed to the Russian occupation and to all the ultra-modern paraphernalia of the Great War of Domination. The only feature about this particular gyro that had startled the Quichua man was its jet black paint job and the dreaded symbol of a Russian eagle with a golden cycloptic eye emblazoned on both sides of its hull. This meant that its pilot was an armed agent for the Military Security Guard. Such agents only showed their colors like this when they were intent upon the official business of making an arrest. For the Indian shuffling along toward the turn in the dusty road, the appearance of the sinister little ship meant that his "game" was up.

The dark-skinned gyro-pilot worked leisurely and methodically. He raised his binoculars from his quarry to the country beyond. Here below was the last of the hills. The scrubby *montania* of the Bolivian *Oriente* began to take shape in this section. Beyond this point he saw the jungle's green mat stretch hazily away under wandering flat clouds, broken here and there by glistening stretches of the shallow Rio Grande. He knew that somewhere out there, not too far distant, was Santa Cruz.

He slipped his binoculars into their case and spoke into a radiophone, "Security scout 13-6-32 calling Zone Seven," he said in Russian, "SS 13-6-32 calling Santa Cruz, over..."

"Zone Seven Headquarters to SS 13-6-32," came a sharp reply. "State your mission. Use code three. We are alerted."

The pilot flipped a switch on his transmitter, which set an automatic speech jumbler into operation. "Coded dispatch to Zone Seven," he announced. "Zone Six Security requesting liaison assistance in connection with the arrest of an enemy agent now in your territory. Name, Stephen Germain. Nationality, U. S. A. Disguised as a Quichua, *Paceno* type. Identification record filed at Cochabamba revealed that he is licensed to travel to Vallegrande for induction into rubber exploitation work, to be assigned to the *Pando* Indian Labor Division. His apparent objective is your experimental station, however, as well as possible sabotage of the serum plant.

"Subject was detected yesterday by V method fifty-eight. For case evaluation, refer to Espionage Bulletin A-8147. Requires special handling.

"I am going to make the arrest. However, our instructions are to turn this man over to Zone Seven—if taken alive—for custody at Santa Cruz until further orders. Have two of your men meet me to receive the prisoner, I am landing on the road two kilometers west of your Transportation Inspection Office Number Five, position AZ-17. Please confirm."

After a short moment of silence, Santa Cruz answered. "Zone Seven Security Office confirms your requisition. Proceed as planned..."

The pilot turned off his radio. While he loosened his radium pistol in its holster, he smiled grimly at his quarry who was just making the turn in the road.

"Now for the cooking of a prize goose for Nicholas the First," he said, and he bent purposefully over his landing controls...

As SOON as the big bluff at the turn in the road hid him from view of the descending gyro, Germain shooed his burro down an embankment into the woods. He followed for a short distance, making sure that his sandals would show their tracks in the brick-red soil. Then he stopped and took off the sandals, thrusting them into his belt underneath his colorful poncho. He removed his *Paceno* hat and also the poncho, which left only his ragged trousers. His braided black hair and his enigmatic, far-seeing eyes, together with his hooked nose and high cheek bones gave him now more of the appearance of an American Indian, but his sinewy body bore the stamp of a scientifically trained athlete.

"Good luck, Fuzzy!" he said to the burro, slapping its rump hard. Then he reached the road quickly by another route, this time taking care not to make tracks with his bare feet. When he reached the road he heard the rocket-gyro's blades whooping to a stop and he knew he only had seconds to take cover. He scattered the dust of the road as he walked across it, in order to conceal his tracks. Then he grabbed roots and boulders on the bluff and very nimbly scaled it. At the top, he slid for cover under the bushes and then turned around to watch for his pursuer.

At that precise moment the pursuer appeared. He was a big, powerfully built Russian, dark-complexioned, but neat and efficient-looking. He wore the black uniform and shiny black boots and insignia, which identified his special office. In his right hand he carried a radium pistol. He had left his cap in the gyro, probably because he thought its peak might obscure his vision. His hair was crew cut. Germain estimated, from the other's alert, business-like expression that he was nobody's fool.

Which was borne out immediately to be true. He went over to the embankment and listened. He saw the burro's footprints mixed up with the sandal tracks; but he did not follow them. He only listened suspiciously to the loud crashings which the burro was still making as it progressed deeper into the woods.

Slowly, then, he turned his head to look at the top of the

bluff, a fanatical light of triumph in his eyes. Germain knew he had figured that an enemy agent seeking to take cover would not be accompanying such a racket. He would, logically, seek hiding in an opposite direction.

As the Russian found a place to climb the bluff, Germain put on his sandals and hastily sought a good point of vantage for making an ambush. It was his only defense. He remembered the knife he had seen in the other fellow's belt. The air was hot. The bushes were full of ticks, which were dropping on him. His pulse raced with an uncontrollable excitement. He swallowed, hard. He knew that this hand to hand fighting between two highly trained veterans—the stakes being life itself—could be an awfully ugly mess. But this was it. This is what they had trained him for at the Strategic Services College. First objective: disarm the enemy...

He soon found a good place beside a small storm gully where he reasoned the Russian might pass. He hid behind a screen of bushes and waited, trying to suppress his heavy breathing, listening, thinking, thinking...

Somewhere in Germain's ancestry was a full-blooded Sioux Indian woman, and that particular squaw had loaned her great great grandson an Indian's face. On just such things as these is destiny hung, for this had been one of the last deciding factors in his having been chosen to imitate a Bolivian Quichua. Certain special diets and other treatments had deepened the color of his skin beyond detection. He knew Quichua from previous adventuring and gold-prospecting days in Bolivia and Peru, as well as some of the difficult Aimara. So here he was, an agent of U. S. Strategic Services, infiltrated into Russian-held territory on a very difficult assignment. His general background as a veteran foreign news correspondent coupled with his training at Strategic Services was a double factor that was supposed to help him out in circumstances such as this. But now he was wondering to just what extent.

"They must think I'm pretty stupid, though," he told himself, under his breath, "to figure I'd not be wise enough to what that gyro was doing on my tail. I knew ever since I passed that fancy detector-ray gadget at the clearance gate out of Vila Vila that something had slipped up. I've got my pass. I've got my identification tag and am carrying no equipment an Indian shouldn't have. But somewhere there's been a slipup, and I'd give a week's furlough in California to know what it is." His brows closed in over his glittering, black eyes in a pensive frown. "But I've got to get through to that damned experimental station and hash up Doctor Borg's serum factory—or bust!"

"Ochen korosho!" called the Russian, suddenly. "If you want to play games, Mister Germain, how do you like this!"

BLUE-WHITE spheres of flame burst all about him, reducing the bushes and trees to ashes where the explosive radium bullets struck. Small rodents squealed in the underbrush. Then—silence.

"You must not hide from me," the Russian continued, coming closer up the storm gully. "It makes me very nervous."

Germain only remained motionless and silent. He could see the Russian now, walking tall and arrogant, looking about him expectantly. In another moment he would pass within a few feet.

"Come, let's give up this little game," the Russian persisted, in fair, over pronounced English. "It is hot out here, and soon it will be time for supper. You don't want to—"

Crack! Germain's foot kicked the Russian's gun hand, which sent the deadly weapon flying. But in the split second that followed he noted something he had not counted on and it checked his charge. The Russian had foreseen such a trick, because he had tied the gun to his wrist. It bounced at the end of the short cord and he caught it deftly, firing at the same instant.

Germain was running for his life in the dense brush, while globes of flame blasted the roots out of the jungle around him. He ran for a certain *arroyo* that he had passed on the way. It was not far. There were big boulders there, in a twisting canyon. Plenty of cover.

The Russian was not firing any more, nor was he making speeches. He was running silently after him. Somewhere, sometime within the next minute or so, the score would be complete. So far the Russian had all the points.

Germain found the *arroyo* and rolled down a semi-cliff, picking up several bone bruises on the way. He scurried behind a boulder and waited again. The Russian arrived and clattered down into the canyon without a moment's hesitation. He grinned derisively and took up a position against a granite cliff wall where he could see several feet in either direction.

"Somewhere within my range you are hiding," he said. "You think you are very smart, you famous American correspondent, but I don't think so. You are hiding behind one of these rocks. If you do not come out with your hands up I shall wait patiently until you reveal your position, and then you will die. It is quite simple."

Once, Germain heard by the sound of the other's voice that his head was turned in another direction. So he peeked quickly at him and ducked back. He knew that the Russian was standing only fifteen feet from him, leaning against that granite wall.

In Germain's mind a desperate, long chance plan took shape. It involved the intervening distances between several giant boulders that lay between him and the Russian, some very silent footwork. Careful listening and timing—and an old, old trick that was so naive that it was not even in the books. It was a silly child's trick, but it had to work, because there was nothing else. With a prayer, he removed his sandals.

The Russian, confident of his advantageous position, and mindful, too, of the additional assistance that would soon be arriving, began to talk again. Actually, it was a deliberate attempt to give Germain a false sense of security.

"You know," he said, "I can't understand why your Democratic Nations do not surrender to us. We have conquered the world, of course with some small help from our Asiatic allies, but always under the guiding genius of Nicholas the First. And incidentally, Mr. Germain, you may be privileged to see our great dictator sooner than you imagine. He is very anxious to meet the man who slandered him with hideous lies in all the democratic newspapers of the world. You Americans forget that freedom of the press is a form of social degeneration. But—"

To his right, twenty feet down the canyon, he heard a small pebble clatter. He fired in that direction, then, startled, he turned and fired in another. But it was too late. The child's trick of the pebble had distracted him just long enough. Something not so childish followed. A boulder, measuring about ten inches in diameter, caught him squarely in the face, smashing his head into a spurting pulp against the cliff. His body slumped to the ground, gun loose in a limp hand. Silence… A hawk circled overhead, high up. Deep in the woods, the frightened chirp of a bird.

Germain, singed by a wave of hot air which blasted off the rock from the radium shell's explosion, picked himself up painfully. Wryly, he looked around the boulder at the dead Russian.

"Jumpin' catfish!" he muttered. He went over and picked up the gun and then turned quickly away.

SOMETIME later he crossed the road again and put on his poncho and his *paceno* hat. He found the burro deep in the woods. Before going on, he sat down on a tree stump to take a rest. It seemed to help, somehow, to talk to the burro.

"We've got to do it, Fuzzy," he said. "Got to get through, even though it'll be tougher sledding now that they're gunning for me. If we don't get hold of the secret of this energy serum that Borg makes for the Russians and the slant-eyes, we're done for, unless we want to go in for a round of atomic bombs. But that's useless, outlawed, mutual suicide."

For long minutes he sat and rested. His thoughts went beyond his immediate goal to greater ones, which lay beyond the war. No nationalist, Germain. He had dreamed of universalism, of Utopian security and positive freedom for all Mankind, emancipation from the blinding slavery of continuous labor and dedication to the higher task of bettering mind and soul, so that henceforth Wisdom might rule over Ignorance and Brutality. He had once believed these things to be possible. As a news correspondent and editorialist he had tried to fight for them.

Yet now it seemed that such dreams were farther from the possibility of realization than ever before. The New World State of the Russian Dictator, Nicholas the First, had Europe, Asia and Africa in its grip, as well as a substantial part of South America. But this was no Utopia. It had turned out to be neither communism nor socialism. It was just another Hitlerian megalomaniac dream of conquest. It was subjugation and hopelessness. The Democratic Nations were writing the darkest pages of their history.

"No!" he exclaimed, slamming his fist into his palm so suddenly that the burro shied away from him. "We've still got to beat them at their own game! Counter espionage and counter invention. If we don't fight now, there will soon be nothing left to fight for."

He spat out the forgotten chunk of coca from his mouth and wrinkled up his nose. "What lousy stuff. This fake coca is worse than the real drug." Then his hard expression drifted away, revealing a man besieged by loneliness. "Sometimes I'm tempted to take the real stuff," he muttered, bitterly. He thought of his wife, Lillian, whom he had left in California. He had not been able to communicate with her since being infiltrated here one year previously.

He heaved the long, lonely sigh of a man who knows how to appreciate a good woman. And he wondered, deep down in, if he would really ever see her again. His chances were narrowing down. A captured spy had never been worth very much, he reflected.

"But there are ways and means," he said, getting to his feet. "Come on, Fuzzy. Let's pull some woods in behind us..."

THE old Pan American-Grace Airways airport hotel at Santa Cruz was now Zone Seven Headquarters for the Twelfth Russian Army. Everything was quite suitable. Ample quarters for officers, with hot and cold running water, refrigeration, fresh meat and vegetables—great luxuries for the jungle country. The local *hacenderos* had enjoyed a good farming season. The cattle were fat and numerous. The sleepy town, still topped with ancient red tiles, was restfully picturesque. Moreover, the *senoritas* were still as pretty as tradition had always claimed.

But this was also a remarkable hideaway for secret experimenters such as the famous Doctor Borg, as well as for such a strategic industry as the manufacture of serum, which was vital to the progress of the dictator's armies. From

Arequipa, Peru, on the west coast, clear to Montevideo, Uruguay, on a line running through La Paz, Cochabamba, Trinidad, Santa Cruz, Puerto Suarez and Asuncion, the Russian forces held South America firmly. North of the La Paz-Asuncion line, with the exception of such seasonally accessible clearings as Concepcion, San Ignacio, San Jose, Robore, and the like, stretched the greatest natural barrier in the world—tens of thousands of square miles of wild, scrubby jungle and swamps. The Russians, themselves, would not cross that in their next great advance. They would go around it, up through Peru, taking Lima and the oil fields at Talara, and on the east coast they would make Sao Paulo their first major objective.

So Santa Cruz was fairly immune to enemy infiltration. It was for this reason that Doctor Borg had chosen this spot in which to carry on his vast, secret experiments, as well as for the fact that the center of the South American continent seemed to be as far removed as possible from certain inimical influences in Asia which he feared much more than the Americans. But that was an inner secret of State which he shared only with Nicholas the First and three others.

At Santa Cruz, few of the men and officers pretended to know what was kept in many of Dr. Borg's long sheds and bomb shelter like control cells. If they were aware of human disappearances around town or if they had heard wild, maniacal shrieks at night they were wise enough to keep their mouths shut and consider themselves fortunate to be on the conquering side of the fence.

BIG, fattish Major Sergeyev Pavlovich winked one bushy-browed eye at his important guest and invited the latter to some more vodka, with an affected gesture of his meaty hand. "So we are letting them believe that the Grand Attack is scheduled for January?" he said. "Ho! Ho! That is a good one, Colonel, when we shall actually attack them in December!"

Tall, gaunt old Colonel Andrew Golovinsky was also well pleased. His medals tinkled merrily as he chuckled and curled one end of his prodigious gray mustache about his index finger. "They also have little information, it seems, concerning the plans of the Mongolian airborne armies. These latter will move *en masse,* you might say, to Central America, concentrating on Panama and Mexico simultaneously. After that, we shall entrench ourselves and make ready, in six months' time, to drive upon the United States' homeland."

Pavlovich's brown eyes flashed genuine enthusiasm. When he became excited his brows closed in over a big, hairy wart that grew between them, and his fat nostrils flared redly. "Then will the decadent Democracies realize," he said, "that they were too slow to relinquish their accursed capitalism and accept with open arms the wise doctrines of Nicholas the First!"

"You speak the words of a true Russian soldier, my good Sergeyev," said the old colonel, looking at the other out of pale, blue-gray eyes. Then he looked up and gazed momentarily in admiration at a brilliantly colored macaw that had just alighted on the roof of the hotel. It was comfortable here, and heavenly warm, he thought even in the shade as they sat in the patio in the late afternoon. It imparted to him a glowing sense of wellbeing. This was a great relief after the cold, thin air of lofty La Paz on the *Alto Plano*. With a barely audible sigh of contentment, he took out a silver snuffbox and proceeded to snuff a few delightfully bitter grains up his nose.

"But tell me, Colonel," said Pavlovich, with an air of ambitious hospitality, "You did not come down off the *Alto* just to visit, I am sure. What else is new? Why, for example, are we alerted in this God-forsaken outpost?" The allusion to God was a figure of speech, as all new World State fanatics were atheists, by political rather than philosophical doctrine.

Colonel Golovinsky took off his monocle and polished it methodically. "That is something I can't tell you," he said, with official secretiveness. "The whole thing is—ah—quite surprising, or at least it will no doubt be for you. But nothing to worry about, really. On the contrary—"

At that moment, an orderly clicked into the patio and saluted. "Your pardon, sir. An operations report from Security." He flipped out the paper and stood like a statue.

"Hmmm," said Major Pavlovich, "what have we here?" He took the sheet and waved the orderly off with a lazy salute. Then his eyes suddenly widened. "What's this? An enemy agent!"

The colonel was only mildly surprised. "You knew we were experiencing some infiltration during the past few years, over the *Alto*, out of Lima," he remarked.

"But they were caught and shot!" said the major, incredulously. "This one almost made it to Vallegrande! Ye Gods! And with Borg's project wide open here. Somebody should have tipped us off sooner. If the Americans ever found out how to produce our energy serum alone they would cost us another year of effort. And if they succeeded in sabotaging the serum plant..."

"You will find considerable information in the General Espionage Manual supplements," said the colonel. "This particular agent has been in Bolivia for a considerable time. Our Security Command Headquarters have been trying to trace him for months. He is very clever, I understand. They had to lead him into ambush, so to speak."

"Hmmm. Not so clever," said the major, still perusing the report. "Method fifty-eight. Ha! I know about that. He was chewing fake coca. How does that treated coca really work under the detector rays? Perhaps you could enlighten me on the entire strategy of the system. There are so many new things. It is difficult to keep up to date out here."

THE colonel was pleased to explain. "When Dr. Borg and his serum plant came to Zone Seven," he said, "the whole area became critical. We knew there would be renewed attempts at enemy infiltration. The most obvious disguise would be that of an Indian, although a really professional job would be difficult to detect. One characteristic common to all the Indians was the coca habit. This is as invariable as their thirst for *chicha*. As through ignorance and poverty they fail to provide themselves with the necessary vitamins, their systems seem to crave a substitute, just as a dog will eat dirt in an attempt to satisfy a vitamin deficiency. So all the Indians must have coca, *para darse valor,* as they say. It is universally traditional, even among the children.

"It was a simple step to place coca under the *estanco* or government reserve control, and then it became a simple matter for us to 'prepare' the coca with a tasteless ingredient which was very slightly radioactive. Their bodies get saturated with the stuff. Of course it kills them off in a few years, but we shall not be requiring Indian labor here much longer, and the increased death rate is in conformity with World State's policy of population reduction, that is, with the exception of the Slavic races, of course. These latter must be increased to outnumber the Mongolian races, as our wise leader has foreseen that complete security will not be ours until we have dominated the yellow men as well. However, the chief current value of this treated coca is for security against espionage, as has been borne out so successfully in case of Stephen Germain.

"The new detector rays at Vila Vila are different than

ordinary ones. As each Indian passes them, the operator hears a little buzz that identifies the radioactivity in his body. Naturally, an intelligent, self-respecting agent will never take habitually to real coca because even the untreated variety dulls the mind. So when Germain passed the rays and did not produce a buzz, the operator reported it to Zone Six Security. Security allowed him to continue, under observation, to see what direction he would take. As had been suspected, he did not take the direct branch to Vallegrande, but continued toward Santa Cruz. This is catching him red handed, even as an Indian, because it's in violation of his forged license."

Pavlovich looked at the report. "I see a Zone Six Security Guard was to make the arrest at 2100. That was about an hour ago. Two of our own guards went out to receive the prisoner. That is good. But why do you suppose he is to be held here for custody?"

"You will find out. All I can say is that it would have been worse than you think to have an enemy agent operating freely in our midst this week."

"Why, colonel?"

"I repeat that I am not permitted to tell you, Major, but you will soon know." The colonel got up out of the green lawn chair and groped in his inner shirt pocket for a Brazilian cheroot. "You will find out tonight," he said, striking up a flame from his lighter. "At about four hundred."

"Four hundred—that's midnight!"

"Correct, Major Pavlovich. It would be advisable to stand by on the alert." The colonel wallowed luxuriously in a dense halo of cheroot smoke...

THAT night near midnight Major Pavlovich knew, at least, that the colonel's deep secret involved a transoceanic jet plane. This much Radar had already told all observers in Zone Seven. Security reported that the ship was cleared through special channels. The Security officer in charge appeared embarrassed, but he said he was under orders from Security Command at La Paz not to reveal anything about the strange ship's mission. However, Major Pavlovich saw that the fellow's unusually ruddy face was pale with suppressed excitement.

"Hell," Pavlovich told him, smashing out a cigarette with his boot heel. "Take it easy. As long as we're not in for a raid—which I didn't think anyway—nothing else is worth foaming at the mouth about."

"Sir," continued the officer, "we are worried about our two operatives who were dispatched to bring in the American prisoner, Stephen Germain. They should have returned two hours ago. There has been no sign. I haven't any other aircraft at my direct disposal. Perhaps—"

Pavlovich was impatient. He had begun to suspect the magnitude of the event that was to occur at midnight and it had dwarfed all other considerations into insignificance in his mind.

"Stop worrying, will you?" he said. "You can take a couple of my A57-Scout jobs out if you want to. You'll probably find those guys grounded by maintenance trouble. You know that pick-up job of yours is an old clunker, I never did like those old-fashioned turbine gyros. Give me a report in the morning. I'm busy!"

He went out to the airport, hastily wiping sweat off his fat brow. He was vaguely aware that he had not acted quite efficiently in this matter, but all other matters of office had to wait until he attended properly to this affair which was about to occur. He was beginning to have an idea of who his visitor might be, though he could hardly dare to hope. He straightened his tie and had a look at his uniform, while his husky heart began to pound.

There in the passenger compound, talking to Colonel

Golovinsky, was Dr. Borg, dressed in tropical white. The way he waited, you could tell he knew what was going to happen.

"Good evening, Major," he said. "You look as though you shared already the excitement of this glorious occasion with us."

The doctor was a shrunken man with a big, grizzled head, a pockmarked face and a clay-like complexion. When he grinned it was more like a toothy snarl. It was difficult to take to the fellow. Little things about him rubbed you the wrong way. The ever-present sparse stubble on his chin, for example, which he never seemed to shave down completely, and the way his left eye twitched and made itself smaller than the other. His big, warty hands with purplish veins, the right one always grasping the ivory nut skull head of his silver-tipped iron-wood cane. And his crooked limp. He was a famous but an ugly man.

The major had no further time for contemplation of Dr. Borg, for the giant jet plane swooshed majestically overhead. A vast, blacked-out bird, wings slanted sharply back for supersonic velocity, now flashing a fiery, cycloptic eye at them as it maneuvered to pick up the landing beams. Lights, signals and active ground crews suddenly filled the warm, tropical night.

"Here she comes," he said, and waited.

When the plane door opened and its interior companionway lights flooded the platform of the passenger ramp, Major Pavlovich knew that the incredible had happened. For there, in all his authoritative person, was none other than Nicholas the First, Dictator of most of Eurasia, the most powerful ruler the world had ever seen, founder-to-be of the world's first universal government. Here, in little Santa Cruz, way out in the Bolivian jungle. For the first time in his life the major felt like fainting.

The reception light beaming from the hotel tower took in the passenger ramp and fully illuminated all figures emerging from the ship. A lieutenant general and two colonels followed Nicholas the First. Shining boots, immaculate uniforms, gold braid, jeweled medals and campaign colors swarmed like a sea from the doorway, followed by the gravely groomed civies of men of state and the shining spectacles and bald heads and portfolios of special aides.

While a twenty-one rocket-gun salute sent blue-white flashes at the starry sky and frightened thousands of jungle creatures into the darkest recesses of their lairs, Nicholas stopped at the head of this avalanche of authority and took a full minute to survey the airport at Santa Cruz. It was the first time that he had ever set foot on the South American continent or filled his lungs with the indescribable air of the tropics. It was, he reflected, the old breath of conquest, but, like love itself, something ever new.

He was comparatively young. Forty-seven was not old for a man who enjoyed the special diets and treatments that were his to command. Barring accidents, he knew he could live to one hundred and fifty. One hundred years left in which to rule the world—*perhaps*. Of late, dark shadows had clouded his bright vision of triumph, ghastly, nightmarish shadows of which he could not speak, except to Borg and three others.

Tall, muscular and trim in his white uniform, with one dazzling ruby and diamond studded Star of Honor on his chest (the highest state award for social contribution, invented by and presented to himself), he cut a figure which was not to be ignored by man or woman. His face, with its sharply trained Kaiser Wilhelm mustache and its short-clipped Van Dyke, was a handsome study in self-justified egotism, a habitual domineering attitude so thoroughly acquired as to be actually regal.

His eyes, above all, bore the mark of all the Napoleons of

history. For here was that rare, complete iciness, which a conqueror must have to march to fame and power across the broken bodies of millions of men, women and children. Here was the self-centered megalomaniac logic which, once more in the bloodied history of Man, could construct and adhere to the fascistic doctrine that the End justified the Means. In the cold, intellectual eyes of Nicholas the First there shone the unmistakable sign of his negative greatness.

COLONEL GOLOVINSKY nudged Major Pavlovich and, with Dr. Borg, they stepped forward. After due saluting, the colonel addressed the dictator.

"Hail Nicholas," he said, gravely. "You do us more than honor by visiting the Twelfth Russian Army in Bolivia."

"I am flattered beyond the power of expression," put in Dr. Borg with a deferential snarl, "for your personal note, which only reached me yesterday advises that you have taken a personal interest in my latest experiments." It was obvious to all that there was something more intimate between Borg and Nicholas than either cared to reveal at the moment.

Nicholas had not moved a muscle, even to answer their salutes. Even when he spoke, his face was a mask. Only his eyes moved, piercingly. His voice was strong, but inhumanly flat.

"Yes, Borg, your experiments alone justified this secret visit. However, there is also something else. You," he said, impaling the major with a stare, "are Major Sergeyev Pavlovich, administrating officer of Zone Seven Headquarters, are you not?"

"At your service, sir!" spluttered Pavlovich, beating out another salute and cracking his heels ponderously. He did not like that cold fish stare.

"What have you done concerning the spy, Stephen Germain?"

"Stephen G——? Oh, yes, sir, the enemy agent of today's report. Why, he should be en route here now, sir, in the custody of a detail which our Security Office dispatched this—ah—afternoon."

Nicholas got icier, while all the austere personages behind him glared disapprovingly at the major. "I have been following coded dispatches on this case on board," he said, eyes blazing. "If you had been doing the same you would know by this time that he has *escaped*. Your Security Office must be having reception trouble or they would know this. Vila Vila has been trying to get you for an hour. Why isn't your auxiliary watch operating if you are under an alert?"

All this even surprised Colonel Golovinsky, and it embarrassed the old officer half way to his grave. As for the major, he seemed to stagger under the blow. But Dr. Borg, who did not appear to belong to the ranks of those who worried too much about authority, was prompted to conversation.

"No doubt," he said, calmly, "the agent will be apprehended before he can do us any harm, sir. After all, such comparatively petty matters should not occupy the attention of one such as your—"

Nicholas stamped one dictatorial boot, and his flat voice went up half an octave. "What do you mean, petty?" he shouted. "Major Pavlovich, I presume by your apparent ignorance of this case that you have also neglected to refer to Espionage Bulletin A-8147!"

For all the unfortunateness of his terrible predicament, Pavlovich remained a soldier. The big, hairy wart between his eyes submerged in folds of sweating skin as his brows came together. His fat nostrils flared out redly. He threw his big shoulders back and said, "Sir, I confess I left that detail to the Security Office."

Nicholas the First shouted, "Guards!"

At his command, two large guards of honor sprang to his side.

"You will deprive Major Pavlovich of all decorations, as well as the insignia of his rank," said the Dictator.

In the entire airport of Santa Cruz there was no sound except the undertones of night wind sighing through the bordering jungle. Major Pavlovich felt his life unexpectedly shattered and crushed, for reasons not fully understood. But he responded in the only way he could. He clamped his big jaw tight and stood rock-steady at attention as his medals and insignia were brutally torn away and stomped on.

"Hell's unholy curse to this bastard of a Stephen Germain!" he thought to himself. "Just when I had a chance of making an impression. Of all people why did this have to happen to me? A thousand cursed damns! If I ever lay my hands on that dirty, foul American—"

"Now," said Nicholas the First, "you will do exactly two things, *Private* Sergeyev Pavlovich. You will go first to the General Espionage Manual and read Bulletin A-8147. Then you will get out of here and never contaminate my vision— unless, of course, you bring me Stephen Germain.

"And if Stephen Germain is brought here," he continued, snapping his attention over to Dr. Borg again, "I order you to use him as your top guinea pig. You wanted a brilliant mind for your final experiment. Doctor, I can assure you that Stephen Germain's is that, though unfortunately somewhat distorted. Perhaps your special surgery will *straighten him out...*"

ONE hour later, in a dull quagmire of unvented rage and despair, Private Sergeyev Pavlovich located Espionage Bulletin A-8147 and read:

"Germain, Stephen: American, born St. Paul, Minnesota, October 30, 1935. Profession, foreign news correspondent

for Chicago Sun Syndicate, until outbreak of the war. Previously invested in Bolivian and Peruvian gold mines. Worked vicinity of Uyuni during period 1955 through 1959. Speaks Spanish and Quichua. Married Lillian Chapman, Chicago, 1966. No children, (Insert: Mrs. Germain has recently enlisted and is attached to the Air-ambulance Corps of the American Sixth Airforce, Caribbean Defense Command.)

"Subject inducted into American army June, 1967. Trained at U. S. College of Strategic Services, Maryland, in preparation for specific mission, infiltration into Bolivia for purpose of acquiring strategic papers and records from Santa Cruz, biological experimentation center which is currently under the direct technical supervision of Dr. Julius Borg. Reported in October as being at large in the vicinity of Cochabamba. It is suspected that he may be wearing the disguise of an Indian, owing to his knowledge of Quichua. All Security Guard offices of Twelfth Army Control Zones Six and Seven are hereby instructed to watch for this man.

"For special evaluation, the following special note is given: As a widely notorious foreign news correspondent and editorialist, Stephen Germain succeeded more than any other American in arousing the displeasure of Nicholas the First. For several years, corruptly unbridled American press entities published this man's vile accusations and insolent slander against the first Dictator of Eurasia, making bold to invent inconceivable lies concerning even the personal affairs of our unimpeachable leader. Nicholas the First has sworn publicly to capture Stephen Germain and attend personally to his justifiable punishment. He has also offered one hundred thousand rubles as a reward for his capture...

"All operatives are warned that Germain is a One-A agent. Any plans for his capture must not be based on presumptions, as Germain is extraordinarily resourceful. This one American agent has killed two of our best counter-agents who were especially assigned to trace him... Special handling. Supplements to follow..."

SOMEWHERE in the still, starlit hours beyond midnight, Nicholas the First and Dr. Borg held a very private conference just between themselves. To any chance eavesdropper who might have understood white Russian, the conversation would have sounded either incomprehensible, or mad, or both.

The meeting took place in the Dictator's private room, the simple facilities of which were far short of what his high level of living in New Moscow had accustomed him to. But he showed in his face that he was far more concerned about matters that had no connection with mundane comforts.

He sat at a large, polished desk which had on it nothing except a common napkin, a cup of coffee, a saucer, a spoon, and a bowl of sugar. He stirred the steaming coffee and looked for a long moment at his companion in fear, Dr. Borg.

Borg, never out of composure, pursed his ugly lips gravely and studied the face of the Dictator. He saw the face of a man who belonged to a rare but monstrous breed. Such men belong to no nation or principle. They belong solely to themselves, or if they perform allegiance to their kind it is only for the nefarious purpose of ill-gotten advancement at the expense of others, even if those others happen to represent Humanity, itself. Such men as he could fool the public into buying billions of dollars of weapons of war even when they were gasping for peace. They could wave their hands magically, before breakfast, changing the price of the world's Commodities, causing empires to tremble and fall, sealing the destiny of presidents and kings. Theirs was the power of an evil god. They did not appear to need a soul.

But here was one—perhaps the leader of them all—who

was afraid of something. He was the bold and arrogant dictator of thirty nations; he was mightier than Hitler or Napoleon or Genghis Khan or Attila. He would make history ring with his name, even though dissonantly. But—he was afraid of something, so afraid that he drank black coffee in the depths of the night instead of sleeping and had to take large doses of energy serum to keep going.

"It is your Achilles' heel," philosophized Borg, unhelpfully. "You reached too far, Nicholas, to guarantee your victory over the Americans. The very creatures with whom you made the treaty have always signified that the greatest rulers in our written history were but clay puppets whose power could have been snuffed out like a candle. How blind and idiotic does Man seem, applying the highest significance to his daily affairs when he walks all his life in the shadow of death at *their* hands. And you and Svenga conceived of making a *deal* with them? It is tantamount to making a pact with Hell. In fact, since we are no longer credulous of the Christian concepts of Heaven and Hell, actually they represent a real Hell, because those fiends cannot be trusted with their own mothers. If Agarthi still holds back its hand out of caution, then these others must be something."

"But," protested Nicholas, "Svenga says that they confirmed agreement with the terms of the pact. If the Americans use a surprise weapon on us, or if our Asiatic friends turn on us with something unexpected which we can't handle, they'll use the ancient ray and annihilate any objectives we care to mention. In return for this guarantee, once I am in complete power over the entire surface world, I shall arrange to give them facilities in the matter of food supplies, raw materials, and furnish them with whatever slaves they may requisition."

"Very beautiful," said Borg, squinting in his irritable, ironic way. "But Svenga the mystic is no statesman, and you can't think of everything yourself. What you failed to realize is that you can't deal with them like you would with any civilized nation on the surface. They live in their foul pits and caverns with poisoned minds. They can think only detrimentally. So any treaty with them would be diametrically disrespected in every point. This desire of theirs to organize and procure new food supplies and an unheard of number of slaves only means one thing. They are preparing for the invasion of the upper world; a thing they have dreamed of ever since they suspected surface Man of knowing anything about science. And Agarthi is unprepared. The man of Agarthi would have been our only hope, but then again, Svenga says that this, so called King of the World is not in agreement with your principles. It's a classical dilemma, which may turn out to be an epic paradox. Your supreme secret weapon you may not need, yet it may destroy you on the very threshold of victory."

Nicholas sweated, but he never lost his hardness. There still remained in his eyes that iciness, still that historical, negative greatness which made him a sinister individual and a man to be reckoned with, in spite of the almost supernatural forces which threatened him. The cold eyes flashed defiantly, almost madly.

"Even *they* may not outsmart us, Borg," he said. "Of course, they may adhere to the terms, but if they do not, perhaps we can prepare a means of escape for ourselves as you have outlined. What you wrote to me was fantastic, but so are *they*. If they ever should dominate the world, I for one don't want to be here. Do you really believe that this experiment of yours will prove to be a way out? Ah, Borg, if you could give me one last ace to put up my sleeve you and I could—"

"And Svenga?" queried Borg, with a knowing, sarcastic

snarl. "And Stoyunin and Smirnovski, your confidential ministers whom you forced to sign the treaty?"

"Oh yes, of course, they will be included also; if you can produce that ace, and *if* it is ever needed."

"It maybe needed," said Borg. He hung his heavy cane on the desk by its ivory nut handle. "Whether or not it can be produced will be proved by experimentation alone. My previous experiments were not successful enough, but now I think I know why. With Germain, if I get to use him, I have reason to suspect that I shall succeed."

Nicholas smiled sardonically. "To think," he said, sipping his coffee through thin, merciless lips, "that the brain of the man who slandered me to one world may prove to be a stepping stone *to another...*"

Then he suddenly noted the polished ivory nut handle of Borg's cane. The enigmatic hollows of the little leering skull glared at him. His own eyes blazed angrily.

"Why don't you get rid of that damned thing!" he shouted.

But Borg and his little death's head only stared back in silence...

CHAPTER TWO
The Man in Disguise

THAT night, out of Lima, Talara, Iquitos, and Manaos, an American commando fleet began to take shape. Each wave of stratoships had been organized for its own specific task, but the work of all of them was so coordinated as to concentrate on one central objective—Russian experimental station, Zone Seven of the enemy's Twelfth Army in Bolivia. Primary objective: Dr. Borg's latest documents, and samples of the too successful energy serum, blitz weapon number one of the war. Secondary objective: to destroy the serum plant, itself...

MAJOR "Slim" Kent turned the Controls of the lead ship over to his co-pilot. "You take her for a while, Lieutenant," he said, looking at the black light illuminated chronometer on the instrument panel. He checked his wristwatch. "I'm going to have a shot of coffee."

"Yes, sir," grinned, the sandy haired co-pilot, whose commando black face almost made his teeth look radioactive. "You and that wonderful nurse. I'm not particularly asking for trouble, Slim, but if I got nicked up just enough to lie in sick bay under her gentle care on the way back I'd say the raid was a success. What a woman..."

Kent good-naturedly rumpled the other's hair as he left his seat. "The nurse happens to be Mrs. Lillian Germain," he said. "Ever hear of Stephen Germain?"

"He was a big time news correspondent, wasn't he? What ever happened to him? Get bumped off?"

Kent looked out pensively at the stars a long while before he answered. "I don't know," he said, finally. He cracked his knuckles, something his men were used to when seeing him work under pressure.

"Friend of yours?"

"Yes. We grew up together—all three of us."

"You mean Germain and the nurse?"

"Yes, and it's been a long time since the two of us have seen Germain. Over a year now. He's in O. S. S., operating in Bolivia. You missed the last minute briefing I gave the huskies tonight only got the dope ten minutes before take-off. One of our side objectives will be to look over any possible prisoners at Santa Cruz to see if we can find him…"

"Is he that good?"

"Top rank. His assignment has been the same as ours is tonight. But he has been only one against all of them, and since he started out the objective has become much more important to us. Tonight we're moving in to help him out." Kent turned then and left the cockpit. As he stepped through the companionway he took out his pipe for a last smoke before the bell rang calling everybody to their battle stations.

LILLIAN GERMAIN looked up cheerfully as Kent stepped into the galley. Secretly, she was glad that the two other volunteer nurses had gone forward, because she wanted to talk to him alone.

She rubbed a white forearm across a tearful eye. "You *would* like onions on your hamburgers," she laughed. "I'm ruining my mascara!" The "mascara" in this case was the commando black which covered her entire face. Everybody on board was "blacked out" for the raid.

"The streaks make good camouflage," Kent grinned. "Do you good. Thanks for the chow, Lil. I see you guessed I was too busy at base to mess with the men. Will you guzzle a java with me?"

When they were seated in a tight little galley booth over coffee and hamburgers she stared out of her blackened face with big, blue-green eyes and said, "How soon will it be?"

"What? The arrival? Oh, we'll be jetting down out of the stratosphere in about another half-hour. At that time I'll have to get into the saddle again," he looked at the raven black sheen of her hair in silence. He always found a sort of stability for his thoughts when in her presence.

"Michael," she said, using his real name instead of the more casual "Slim." "You know why I volunteered to be in with the other girls in the first wave of the raid tonight. Tell me, is there any latest O. S. S. information you have on him?" She searched his face, hopefully.

Kent slowly stirred his coffee and looked at her with a wistful grin. "I wish there were two of you instead of one," he said. "Then I'd know what it's like to have a real woman's love like yours, Lil. I've watched you during the long time he's been gone. I've been close to you, too close at times. But you've never faltered. Your thoughts were as unwavering as a birddog's nose, right on him."

Lillian surveyed her companion fondly. She saw a rugged, mannish face topped by kinky, rusty-red hair, a symbol of his virile and tenacious personality. In his calm, gold-flaked brown eyes she read generosity and loyalty. The mustache and pipe seemed to be the logical accoutrements of his nature. Kent was a man and a soldier's idea of an officer.

She smiled in appreciation of his understanding. She knew, from childhood, that he loved her, but that the soft strong silvery chain of friendship had always formed a barrier more impenetrable than steel. For if Kent loved her he worshipped Germain with almost religious fervor.

"Thanks, Michael," she said softly. "I guess I'll always thank you for your understanding and consideration."

Kent took a long drag at his coffee and then got down to business. "I do know something else about Steve," he said, briskly. He was like that. He could take just so much of

Lillian's tenderness, and then he would purposefully fend it off by being abrupt. "The latest information on him is only a day or so old. I got the dope only ten minutes before takeoff and only got to brief about half of the huskies on it. Steve got a message through from Cochabamba saying that he was entering the last phase of the operation. That means—"

Lillian's eyes widened with hope. "That means," she said quickly, "that he might really be in Santa Cruz by now!"

"Don't hope too much, Lil. The going is tough and Steve works as carefully as a master craftsman. He can't rush things like that. However, if they captured him he might be there. We'll certainly have a good look around, anyway."

Lillian suddenly plucked out a handkerchief and hid her face in it. She trembled, and Kent heard soft sobbing sounds that shook him like an earthquake.

"Take it easy, Lil honey," he said. "Let's wait and see what happens."

"Oh Michael," she sobbed. "When will Man ever get through destroying himself in useless warfare? When, oh God, will peace and happiness ever come to us? Kill! Kill! Kill! Is that the only destiny we have? I want a home and Stephen and children and peace and security. These are the simple things that make life livable, but in this accursed world it seems that such things are too much to ask for."

IN THE midst of a deep drag on his pipe, Kent thought of the pre-war Lillian, her tall, cool whiteness, her artistic, neat way of dressing, her love for blue colors, and her passion for flowers; the single dimple that she always used to have on the left side of her expressive mouth—that little natural beauty mark which disappeared the day Germain left and had never returned.

He pushed away his coffee. "The world," he reflected seriously, "is in a hell of a mess, and you know as well as I do that we're in danger of really being taken over by the enemy. This is the darkest moment in the history of the democratic nations. We're fighting against great odds, Lil."

"Yes. The world is a mess because Man is a stupid fool."

"Perhaps. But I think it's more than just that. I can never forget those great editorials that Steve used to write. His main theme was always: Don't die for a flag; live for it. All nations should unite against Ignorance, which is the common enemy. His words used to ring like a liberty bell. He is a great man. He should be using his talents as a statesman. The world needs such leaders now more than ever. I hope to God he'll come back to us soon.

"Steve argued that our great technological advancements have added something new to Man's history and because of this fact history has no way of repeating itself according to previous standards. It's all a brand new situation never experienced before, and what people fail to realize is that a new type of *thinking* is necessary."

Kent had forgotten the remainder of his food. He was warming up to his favorite subject, Germain's philosophy, while his eyes stared into space at the logical world of a universalist. "In every great era," he continued, while Lillian now listened more calmly, aided by a cigarette, "when civilizations or continents have risen or fallen, we have had *original thinkers* who could detach themselves from the vicious circle of stereotyped perspective and point out, in the midst of folly, the true road to follow. But in this terrible time when we need those wise men to guide us more than ever before, where are they? Whom have we had at our international round tables who could think beyond the private or national ambitions represented by their briefcases? Or who, if there have been thinkers, has had the courage to stand up for his convictions and risk his life for them, if necessary? If we had had men like that twenty-five years ago we'd be well launched on the road to Utopia right now.

"Man failed to realize that the World State will come, even in spite of Man owing to fundamental laws operating in the evolution of human society. But he had a choice, twenty-five years ago, a choice between arriving at World Government rationally and peacefully, or through violence and destruction. Now that first choice is gone. We find Nature, itself, establishing the World State. It was inevitable that if Man failed to think, this upheaval should come and that one part of the world should conquer the other part. Modern technology made nationalism and production for profit as outmoded as feudalism.

"People without recourse to thought have thrown every label in the book at Steve. But he's neither communist nor fascist. He is a realist, a fundamentalist. He can see the handwriting on the wall. He can see that some new world *ism* is necessary for Man to get along. The democracies, he said in one editorial, have tried too long to use a Model T Ford carburetor on a 1960 Lincoln. It just doesn't work. In Nature, fundamental law says that the species must adjust itself to environment. If the species cannot adapt itself, it perishes.

"The Russians are not desirable world rulers, nor is any one nation or race particularly endowed to rule over Mankind as a whole. Nicholas the First, with his own personal *ism*, which leaves the dreams of the great Russian thinkers shattered in its wake, will always be a tyrant. We will be biological cells of his state. But he became the ruler, good or bad, over thirty nations because he abided by the fundamental of adjustment, in this case adjustment to machine-age environment-production for use rather than *profit*. We have not. It has been a hellish mistake."

Just then, a bell rang. Lillian looked frightened.

"Michael," she said, griping his hands.

"This is it," he said, quietly. "Just remember the training you've had, Lil. I'm going now. Go to your post. We'll be diving through their radio shells in about ten minutes. Landing in half an hour. Good luck…"

"Michael…"

"Yes?" He had stood up and was hastily knocking out the ashes from his pipe.

Lillian came close to him. "This is just in case—and for old times' sake."

Kent, for a brief, flaming moment, gathered her in his arms and kissed her. Then he left her without looking back.

IN THE scrub jungle west of Santa Cruz the two searchers sent out after Germain from Zone Seven paused suddenly and listened. Far away to the east they heard the mournful wail of sirens. From their position on the bank of a low hill they could see searchlights fencing at the menacing sky.

"A raid!" exclaimed one.

"The damned Yankees!" cried the other.

"Where in hell did they come from?"

"They must have got wise about Nicholas."

"Damn…I hope we wipe them out."

"We probably will…"

NOT far from this place, Stephen Germain also listened and looked at the sky, but with opposite emotions. "Lord. What a sensation," he exclaimed, under his breath. "To feel the presence of American forces again…" He wondered wistfully if his old friend Kent might be in the raid. "No, that's too much to ask for. Damn! If I had only accomplished my mission sooner I might have been there to get on board and go back with them. Wouldn't *that* be something…"

Just then he saw something in the sky that set his heart pounding. He could not believe his eyes. He thought, for one tortured moment that his imagination was pasting mirages on the starlit sky. At first it was just a lesser darkness against the stars. But it mushroomed out. He saw several of them, widely dispersed.

"Parachutes!" he cried, half aloud. "Yankee raiders..." He knew that these were the task group to take over the few highways that led to Santa Cruz. They would have collapsible jet cycles. These he could see falling attached to other parachutes. They would ride in toward the objective, bombing the road and shooting up any possible sources of reinforcements.

As a commando plunked into the bushes not fifty feet from him, a breath-taking possibility took shape in his mind. *Transportation to Santa Cruz!* By making a mad dash, a jet-cycle could make it in considerably less than an hour. The dead Russian's gyro was out of the question. Without equipment it would be a clay pigeon for automatic radar and radio shells. Moreover, he had left it far behind him by now and a lot of Russians had been beating the bush for him back there.

So, with extreme caution, he began to stalk the commando. The radium pistol he had picked up from the dead Russian had turned out to be empty of ammunition and he had discarded it. But the commando would have a heavier weapon, which he needed if he was to join the raid. Stealthily, he crept up to within ten feet of the fellow. He could see him struggling to get out of his harness and it did his heart good to hear some clear cut Yankee cusswords here in the enemy's territory where he had spent one year going it alone.

"Hey buddy!" he shouted. Then he dashed silently to another spot.

It was well he did so because after a moment's dark silence

an electric machine gun with explosive bullets reduced his previous location to smoking, cleared real estate—a new cabin site in the jungle. The commando had freed himself. He melted into darkness. But Germain knew he was still close by.

"I'm American!" he yelled, and he jumped again. But the explosive bullets did not come this time. Perhaps, he thought, the commando did not want to reveal his position by firing, suspecting that he was contending with the enemy, as most Russians spoke English these days.

"Don't shoot," he shouted. "Hang up your flashlight and hide where you want to. I'll walk into the light with my hands up."

The woods produced a deathly silence. Germain was thinking a thousand troubled thoughts. Had the fellow run off and left him? Or was he the cold-blooded, precision type veteran who always shot first and argued later? He probably was. Maybe he was stalking him down at this moment. He cursed under his breath and grabbed dirt. He snaked away on his belly, slowly, looking back, around, everywhere, listening and waiting, as tense as a thousand springs.

Then, like a light from Heaven, he suddenly saw the flashlight, and he heard the bushes rustle as he moved back away from it. It lay in a tree crotch, pointing right at him.

"Get into the light," said a rather nervous voice. "And hands up—no funny business."

HE DID as directed. The commando saw, to his surprise, a ragged Bolivian Indian walk into the beam of light, his empty hands high above his derby-like hat.

Immediately, he got up out of his crouching position and came forward, sub-machine gun still tightly clutched and ready. He grabbed his flashlight and shone it in Germain's face.

"What the hell…" he said. "How come an—Indian like you can talk English? You're not an Indian, maybe. In fact—" The commando's eyes widened in an expression of surprise. "Hey!" he exclaimed. "What's your name?"

Germain changed his voice to the short-clipped tones of a commanding officer. "I am Captain Germain," he said, "attached to O. S. S. I'll have to have your gun and a cycle to get to Santa Cruz at once."

"This is the damnedest coincidence I ever heard of," the young commando replied. He was chewing a large wad of gum, which he came near to swallowing. His eyes glistened excitedly. "You fit the description all right. You're damned lucky we've been told about you, but our orders are to get you to one of the pick-up ships in the third wave. Sorry, sir, no gun."

"You mean one of the objectives was to pick me up?"

"Sure. Major Kent briefed us on that, and—"

"Kent?" cried Germain. "Don't tell me you mean 'Slim' Kent?"

"Sure. C. O. of the whole show tonight. Come on…let's pick up a cycle. I'll ride you in. We've got a helluva lot to do. Two hours for the first wave. Then come the bombers and strafers to wreck the serum plant and hold off Russian reinforcements. Right in the middle will come the pickups. We've got to move fast and snappy…"

CHAPTER THREE
Conflict

PRIVATE Sergeyev Pavlovich crouched in the jungle like an ape. He looked up above him at the patches of stars that he could see through the tangled branches of the scrub trees. Great beams of white light swept the firmament. Huge sirens shook the air with seismic force. He felt the vast sound in his solar plexus. Rocket guns at the airport and in the village batted radio shells skyward at the capacity rate of ten per second. Each one sought its target automatically. In just one minute the night had blasted itself out of a monastic calm into flaming, roaring pandemonium, all of which took him completely by surprise.

For private reasons of his own he carried a heavy calibre piece of equipment which he had stolen. It was a deadly Russian supersonic projector fed by a generating unit on his back. It had an effective range of only one hundred yards, somewhat like an old-fashioned flame-thrower, but all he asked of life at the moment was to get within one hundred yards of Stephen Germain, to blast his red corpuscles into sickly, watery protoplasm and return to Santa Cruz with his stinking corpse.

This had become such a mental fixation that even the raid could not be considered for long. "To hell with it," he growled, and he turned his face once more toward the first transportation station on the Vila road. He was taking a short cut to it, under cover, because he knew he would have to steal a roadcar to get to the territory where Germain had last been seen. Pavlovich was *persona non grata,* unassigned, without orders. But nothing mattered to him now. He wanted Germain. That was all.

As he walked onward, still not far from the airport, his path was lighted intermittently by the glare from radio shells exploding high above. He knew that many of the American ships and gliders were being hit, but he also knew that many others were piercing the anti-aircraft resistance by means of interference beams that jumbled the shells' radio guidance so that many missed their otherwise inevitable targets. The damned Yankees, he reflected, were still the smartest ones left.

"But we'll smash them," he told himself, savagely.

Just then a big, crippled sky train came floundering darkly down toward him, looming swiftly, blotting out the whole firmament of stars. It came at him, piling up jungle with a roaring, earthshaking plunge. Pavlovich flattened frantically before the steamroller, while a tree snapped over him, pinning him to the ground.

The large ship was on top of him, held off only by tough, tangled scrub tree trunks and branches. He saw black figures raining down to the ground from the ship all around him, and he lay very still, watching. This, he observed, was a tough, veteran crowd, armed to the teeth.

A muted, dull red light illuminated one operation close to him. Black figures scurried and worried about a large, gadget covered apparatus. He knew that these technicians were setting up a large sonic beam disrupter. It was big enough to disrupt all supersonics in camp. No death rays tonight, he thought, if they get that thing going. It would cover the whole territory, unless someone could prevent its use.

He tried to use his own projector on the operators but he could not reach his generator switch. Then, suddenly, he felt the tingling of supersonic waves, which meant that the disrupter was in operation. Too late. The Russian garrison would have to use straight bombs and gunfire—maybe some gas. This technological warfare, he soliloquized silently, always simmered down to old-fashioned fighting. Too many counter-gadgets. War was primitive no matter how you dressed it up. But, after all, that was the way he liked it. His big muscles ached to get free for some hand to hand commando scuffling. Many an enemy skull had cracked before under his ponderous fists. But he was helpless now. He sweat the sweat of frustration. He almost cried aloud like a child.

Just then a Russian barrage of heavy calibre rocket shells tore the guts out of the woods. The ground jumped around like a chicken coop roof in a cyclone. Unendurable light hammered and flashed on him. Dirt flew at his skin and stayed there, a part of him. He chewed the ground, hoping to live through this blasting. Trees that had been changed to dust snowed on him as though a blizzard was blowing. He heard the cutting screams and gurglings of the crippled and dying mingled with sharp officers' commands. Then— comparative silence, except for muffled moaning sounds, the distant explosion of the radio shells high above, the rapid, deep *pum-pum-pum* of the anti-aircraft guns.

Two figures crept close to him. The sky flashed battlefire, allowing him to catch glimpses of their faces, intermittently. They crept nearer, both of them looking in the direction of the airport, just half a kilometer away.

"It's hell," said the biggest one, adjusting his steel helmet. "But I think we can do it. Their garrison is not any too large, apparently, in spite of the resistance they are putting up for the moment. However, you've got to move your unit back out of rocket range. Seems they got a reading on our ship when it crashed. You move back with the disrupter crew and I'll move up." He spoke into a compact walkie-talkie, "All groups hold fire. Huskies keep moving in. But stay off the field. Techs, keep setting up your artillery. Observers report in three minutes..."

Suddenly, Pavlovich noticed with some surprise that the smaller of the two was a woman. She had crept very close to him, within four feet. He was well hidden by leaves so that she could not see him.

RISING Russian manpower plus the personal philosophies of Nicholas the First had taken Russian women out of the armies and industries and sent them back to the home, or elsewhere, as the state decided, so that during the Great War of Domination the Russian soldier was not as accustomed to carrying his womenfolk to the front line as were the hard-pressed men of the democratic armies. So the appearance of this woman beside Pavlovich in the thick of battle aroused his curiosity.

In the silent patches he could hear her. She was breathing hard from excitement, or exertion, or both. In her tight knuckled hand was a machine pistol. She wore the Red-Cross emblem of a nurse. The scraping of jungle branches had wiped half her makeup away, leaving a white cheek spattered with blood. Half her hair was down out of her helmet, raven-black, splashing like India ink across her shoulder. He lay there admiring her clean-cut profile and the determined set of her chin. He had not known that Yankee women were like that. It was a revelation that tended to undermine some old convictions.

"I'll leave you here," said the officer beside her. "From the sound of these poor devils around us, your unit has plenty of work to do. So long, Lil, and God keep you."

The nurse plucked at his arm. "Michael..." she gasped, afraid for his sake. *"Please* be careful."

"Okay. If you're a good girl maybe I'll bring back somebody you know."

"Oh pray God that Stephen is here," she exclaimed. Then she was left alone.

Stephen—thought Pavlovich, *Stephen Germain!* And "Lil" was for *Lillian.* Pavlovich remembered only too vividly now what he had gone over so painfully in Espionage Bulletin A-8147. He growled inaudibly. So that was it. This dame was Germain's wife! What a combination! If he might get his hands on her, it would at least be half as good as getting Germain, and maybe holding her as hostage would make excellent bait...

At that moment, the weight of the big ship above him shifted slightly. Pavlovich suddenly knew he was free to move...

FOR forty minutes, Santa Cruz was a full-fledged battlefield. The commando raid was on a major scale, but the objective was not protected by a major garrison. Gradually, the Russians appeared to be beaten down. The core of enemy opposition backed into a huge bomb shelter that the enemy seemed to be especially anxious to protect. The Americans went after their main objective, Dr. Borg's papers and his serum. With the booty captured, they began a retreat. They returned to their hidden positions in the jungle and waited, waited for the second wave of bombers and fighters, which would beat off the reinforcements that were no doubt rushing in from La Paz, Cochabamba, Puerto Suarez, Oruro, Uyuni and Asuncion. Before the enemy could concentrate in force, however, the swift jet pick-ups would swoop in by the hundreds and take away the survivors. By that time the time bombs planted in the serum factory would blast the place off the map.

Two things marred Kent's triumph. There was no sign of Germain. And when he returned to the crashed lead ship and the overworked first-aid group of the immediate attachment under his command, Lillian was not to be found. He had searchers out, but so far there were no signs of her. As officer in command he could not look for her personally, but he would have sacrificed his rank to look for her if it had been morally possible at the moment. Twenty minutes to wait before the second wave struck. A lot could happen in that time. And it did.

Suddenly, from the area of the Santa Cruz station buildings emerged about two hundred Russians. They came firing submachine guns, covered by a sparsely distributed rocket-shell barrage.

"Hop-heads!" was the cry along the line.

Kent had seen them personally before in spectacular mass action at the famous Battle of Salta. Russian soldiers shot with the famous energy serum—the miraculous stuff whose secret they had come to get, which he had captured already and was only waiting to carry away with him.

The synthetic supermen dodged and ran like football players, ducking, leaping, making themselves difficult targets. They wore bullet-proof jackets and face-armor, too heavy for normal men to carry, yet they ran like lightning, just like human tanks, firing fast as they came. In little more than sixty seconds they had crossed the open field and jumped into the jungle. From there on it was potshot and hand to hand. But even the tough commandos could not cope with these supercharged men. They were madmen fixed with one idea, to kill or capture. They could break bones with their maniacal grips, even if their own normal bones had to break also under the terrific pressure of their python-like sinews. They smashed through…

However, at this time nobody chanced to take undue notice of two special Russian guards who came after the first advance. They had paused several times to bury certain objects shallowly in the ground in about five places. Then they came running after the rest.

KENT and his immediate detachment, with what they had captured, were rounded up and roughly herded back toward the station. Under the effects of the energy serum no man could serve as a commanding officer, so the Russians always sent with their doped fighters several untreated guards or officers. Two of these, the same two special guards who had buried the objects in the ground, now gripped Kent stiffly, one on each side, and walked him briskly ahead. The super-charged warriors, panting wildly, some foaming at the mouth due to drug reaction, pushed and kicked other American commandos along with them. Kent and the two special guards were out in front.

Suddenly, the guard on his right said in clear, Yankee English, "Run like hell!" just loud enough for him alone to hear.

So Kent ran with the two guards. But they did not let go of him. At one place they pulled him sharply to one side and then ran on again with him. They had gotten a head start.

"What the devil?" Kent puffed, but he still ran, as bullets whistled and the wild Russians shouted. They started to sprint after them in a dense mass, leaving the other American prisoners sparsely guarded.

Then the earth shook. Five times, in blinding flashes, while arms and legs sailed through the air. Kent fell flat with the two guards, while plank-hard sheets of dirt and searing hot waves of blast-force seemed to iron him out.

"Land-mines!" he exclaimed.

"Jumpin' catfish!" said the guard next to him.

Kent suddenly took a startled look at the fellow, whose helmet had been knocked off his head. He saw an Indian with braided hair grinning at him.

"Steve! Steve Germain!" he shouted above the battle din going on above and the shrieks of the dying men behind him. "Where did you—"

"Shut up and run!"

So they got up and ran again, this time not so heavily

followed. They could hear fighting behind them. The straggling Americans now outnumbered their captors, as the latter had taken the main blast from the land mines. Kent sensed that they would all have a chance yet, as this superman charge had been Santa Cruz's last flurry...

AT DR. BORG'S battered administration office, Kent set up emergency staff headquarters. A check-up by radiophone revealed that they again held the upper hand. Everybody was digging in for the impact of the second wave, which was due in a few minutes. Already reports were coming in concerning the multiple approach of heavy enemy reinforcements. It was going to be a big fight yet, although from this point on it would belong primarily to the American bombers and strafers.

"Steve," said Kent, to his old friend when he had his first chance. He grabbed him by both shoulders and looked at him. "How in Heaven's name did you do it? Lord! Is it *good* to see you!"

"It's a long story, Slim," said the other. "I owe a lot to this young commando here." He indicated his smiling companion who had first dropped into sight from the sky. "He deserves it medal..."

"Thanks, Captain!" grinned the commando, wiping his grimy face. "You're not so bad yourself. You thought up the strategy and went straight to the arsenal for those mines. I've never seen such a quick precision kayo job done on sentries before. I'll never forget it, Captain; it was an honor."

"But how come you were able to locate me?" said Kent.

"That was the easiest part of it," grinned Germain. "Just had to make a beeline for the point of resistance that was drawing most of the enemy's attention. And there you were, just like the queen bee." Germain's smile changed to an expression of concern. "You'd better brief me quick on

what's going to happen. But first just tell me one thing…"
As Germain's black eyes searched those of his friend's, a
quiver of wistfulness touched his brow. "How and where is
Lillian?"

Kent's elated expression dropped from his face. His mind
suddenly swam in black despair as he looked back at the
other's face.

"Steve," he said, falteringly. "I've got to tell you that—"

Just then a young lieutenant dashed in. "Pardon, Major
Kent!" he said in uncontrollable excitement. "Sir, we've
struck the jackpot! I mean—we're in great luck, sir. We can't
break into that big bomb shelter yet, but we know who's
there. Got it from some of the prisoners. Nicholas the First
is hiding there with Dr. Borg and a whole staff of Russian big
name officers and confidential aides. He came here on a
special inspection trip and we've trapped him!"

Kent and Germain looked at each other, pale even under
their respective battle-smudge and camouflage. Now,
however, there was too little time for exclamations of
surprise. Minds had to work quickly, in spite of surprises.

Kent gave an order. "Guard that shelter as objective
number one." He turned to Germain as the soldier dashed
out. "We've got to win through tonight," he said. "It might
turn the whole war in our favor if we could capture both the
serum and the Dictator in one grab, *if* he really is there.
Sounds unheard of, but it may be in our hands."

Germain fixed a steady gaze on Kent and said quietly,
"You were going to say something about Lillian…"

Kent's sweating, troubled face looked up suddenly,
listening. A dull rumbling shook the building they were in.
Everybody in the room stood still and listened. Trained ears
analyzed the sounds as distant aerial battle and bombardment.

"It's the opposition," said Kent. "They're fighting the
second wave. Damn it! That's bad. Still, if they fight it out

some place else, the third wave may—"

"Notice something peculiar?" said a strange voice suddenly, in a heavy Russian accent.

They turned and saw a big, grimy Russian climbing in through a blasted window. He had lost his helmet. His black, kinky hair was full of twigs and dirt. On his back was a generator unit, and in his big hands was a supersonic projector. He glowered at them from beneath bushy eyebrows that converged together, half submerging a hairy wart between them.

When he spoke, his nostrils flared redly. "Notice there is no tingle in the air?" he said, covering them all. "Your big disrupter is out of commission, *nyet?* I blew it up. That means I can make pudding out of all of you with this." He gestured demonstratively with the projector. "Also, your second fleet is being slightly exterminated—and your pretty time bombs will be shut off in time to preserve the serum plant. It is no use, gentlemen. The fight is done. You will drop your guns and raise your hands."

Kent, Germain, and three other American soldiers in the room did as they were ordered. They could judge by the sudden commotion outside that the Russians were coming out of hiding with the supersonic equipment. Somewhere a big projector had been set up and placed in action. They heard a few rounds of American sub-machine gun fire, some shouted orders, running feet, other shouts in Russian, then—*zung-g-g!* The deep, belabored hum of a supersonic projector outside brought ghastly stillness to the night, and Germain and Kent felt sickened at the thought of good American blood turning to water under the death ray.

"Which one of you is Stephen Germain?" asked the Russian.

Germain had his helmet back on, which covered his hair, but not his brown Indian's face.

Nobody replied.

"I thought he might be interested," the Russian continued. "I got his wife locked up. Nobody but me knows where."

Germain was strained at the limits of self-control by this astounding statement. Lillian here?

THE almost impossible combination of joy and longing and horror could have broken two ordinary men. But he still restrained himself. Now he knew why Kent had twice hesitated to tell him about her. She had been in some sort of volunteer group with the raid, no doubt. She had been captured. After a year of being away from her and then having her so near—

"She is a good looking dame," the Russian taunted, his feverish eyes fixed knowingly on Germain. At the corners of his mouth showed flecks of spittle, a sign that he was under the influence of energy serum. For one second he looked like a fiend ready to deliver a *coup de grace* to a helpless victim. Then he said, viciously, *"I happen to know."*

Germain sprang forward like a shot from a bow, low down, underneath the supersonic beam. *Zung-g-g!* The beam struck Kent's arm and killed a soldier behind him.

In a fit of maniacal rage, Germain pitted his highly trained body against the supercharged Russian's superior weight. Frothing, Pavlovich dropped the projector and caught him in a superhuman grip, intent upon murder.

At the moment that Kent, with one good hand, painfully picked up his gun from the floor, half a platoon of Russians invaded the place. In a matter of seconds they had everybody rounded up and covered, leaving a cleared space for the fight that was going on. Pavlovich had grunted something at them in Russian, and the corporal in charge stood by hesitantly and watched instead of interfering.

The Russian knew his commando tactics and had a highly

developed repertoire of specialized blows, but he was not as refined at Judo as was Germain. Twice, when it looked as though the American's neck was going to be broken, he recuperated by rolling over and sending the Russian flying against the wall. But the more Pavlovich got beaten up the more effect was brought out of the charge of energy serum he had taken. Bleeding, disheveled and torn, both men charged each other like two jungle cats.

For one brief instant they whirled around in an indistinguishable blur. Then Germain was down underneath Pavlovich. Blindly, Pavlovich tried to reach Germain's throat and cut his windpipe. He gripped his neck with both hands and Kent cried out as he saw Germain's eyes bulge and his face turn purplish red. Then Germain's wiry body went into an amazing contortion and Pavlovich found himself sprawled on his back, tied up in a clinch, with his right arm in a position where Germain could break it.

"Hands up," came a voice that was as cold as Arctic snows. "Break that arm and you die."

Germain, torn and battered, nostrils running blood, and with one eye already swelling shut, looked up from his victim straight into the glacial eyes of Nicholas the First.

The Dictator had made a surprise appearance, followed by Borg, Golovinsky, and what seemed to be a whole company of guards. He trained a beautiful gold-plated Russian radium-pistol at Germain. His uniform was disheveled, but his triumphant carriage made that detail seem a trivial matter. He beamed at Pavlovich suddenly, as strong-armed guards brought the two men to their feet. Iciness gave way in his eyes to glittering enthusiasm.

"So you *did* redeem yourself," he said, in English, so that Germain would understand. "I am told it was you who blew up the enemy's sonic disrupter and inspired this splendid counter-strategy. For this you will redeem your rank. And because you have captured Stephen Germain I shall consider you for the personal reward of one hundred thousand rubles. Colonel Golovinsky!"

"Sir?" The old officer snapped to attention at his side.

"You will please present Major Pavlovich's name for promotion to the rank of Lieutenant Colonel at your next planning council at Command Headquarters, and you may submit my special recommendation, on the basis of persistence of purpose, courage under fire, and leadership and ingenuity becoming an officer."

The colonel, somewhat flabbergasted, saluted and looked dubiously at Pavlovich. The latter's drug spell had subsided as the Dictator spoke. He stood proudly at attention and said, "Thank you, sir!" But he said nothing about Lillian Germain.

THE Dictator's eyes then turned cold again as he faced Germain. "If I know how to give just rewards," he said, in his flattest tone, "I also know how to deal with such depraved enemies as you, Stephen Germain. I have you at last. You may feel complimented that your capture represents to me one of my greatest personally desired objectives, I have in my hands at last the sniveling degenerate who sought to turn a world against me—*me!*" he shouted, tapping his chest. "You will find out that you were trying to cut off the only light of Reason in this sorry world. I am the only savior of Humanity…"

"Hail Nicholas!" chanted the Russian guards behind him.

"It is I, Nicholas," he continued, "who will straighten you all out in your blind, stumbling, erratic paths. This is the world of Tomorrow. It takes cold logic, Mr. Germain, a *very* cold logic, to pick the *right* path to follow. You sick Americans have no leader to tell you what is right. You dance to destruction and racial oblivion in a madhouse filled with leg-shows and jukeboxes. This is a serious era. Since you mismanaged the office of leadership that you once held in this world I had to rise up and take things under my own control. And it is infinitely better, and it will be best of all when I have finished dominating you stubborn, crazy, idiotic Americans!"

Germain figured that spitting in big shots' face belonged to 19th century melodrama, so he fought the urge and remained silent. Another Hitler, was his only mental comment. His mind was still turning over a thousand thoughts in regard to Lillian. To think that she was here somewhere and he was helpless to get to her.

"Dr. Borg!" said Nicholas.

The stooped, dwarfish doctor limped forward. His evil little eyes surveyed Germain as a biologist might look at a prize litter of white mice.

"I hereby make you a present of this prisoner," said the Dictator. "You may do with him exactly as you please. He is your *total* property…"

Nicholas turned and stamped off with his aides and special guards. Several guards detailed to help the doctor took Germain away, followed by Dr. Borg, who evidenced on his ugly face the eagerness of an expectant father. Other guards took Kent in another direction. The latter strained to watch Major Pavlovich, just as Germain was trying to do so, too. They both caught a last glimpse of him as he struck off in another direction with a definitely exultant step.

About them all crescendoed the mournful thunder of war…

CHAPTER FOUR
Guinea Pig

LILLIAN GERMAIN had felt around in the dark closet for something sharp, something that could open her veins before the Russian returned. She was convinced that the raid had failed. She felt that her husband was probably dead— Kent also. She had seen so much of death, especially this night that it seemed to her to be one of the most dependable of all probabilities. And now this Russian who had captured her and knocked her unconscious so that he could smuggle her into this hiding place had her exactly where he wanted her.

When she heard him enter the adobe cottage again, she shrank, nauseated, into a corner. It was cold. She shivered without her jacket. Her limbs ached where she had been manhandled. All that she could think of now, however, was that the brute was back again.

Pavlovich swung the door open, triumphantly, greedily. He reached in and yanked her out, mercilessly. His eyes devoured her tall, perfect figure clad now only in humiliating remnants of clothing.

"We have a little unfinished business," he said, in a tone that was as thick as his lips. He pulled her to him and kissed her neck. Her nails sought vengeance...

Just then someone banged on the door and it swung open. Pavlovich turned in rage to contemplate the embarrassed face of an orderly. The latter looked in amazement at the sight of a beautiful white woman in such an unexpected place and in such disarray. He gazed in momentary fascination at her voluminous, jet-black hair.

"Sorry, sir," said the orderly, after one dazed moment. "Orders from Nicholas the First. He requests your presence."

"Get out!" shouted Pavlovich. "I'll get there in time, man! Don't concern yourself—"

Just then a sergeant stepped up to the door. Pavlovich saw a whole guard platoon standing outside looking in. It was the 5:00 a.m. change of watch.

"Trouble, sir?" said the second man.

"No," Pavlovich replied, more calmly now. This, he thought, could turn out to be a scandal. He knew that word of it would get to the Dictator. As he straightened up his uniform he formulated a quick plan of action. He could not risk disfavor at this stage of the game. In fact, he thought with a growing smile, he knew how to turn this incident to his further advantage.

"Come on, you," he said to Lillian. "Guard detail!" he commanded. "Two of you bring this woman with me."

Nicholas the First sat having his breakfast at a great table in the bomb shelter. As the crowd of attendants and officers parted to admit Pavlovich, he looked up, suddenly aware of Lillian.

He paused in his eating, a choice chunk of toast and egg poised halfway between plate and mouth. The guards shoved her forward.

Nicholas lowered his fork and sat back, surveying her quietly but thoroughly.

"A blanket for the lady," he requested. As a light blanket was thrown around her semi nude form he said to Pavlovich, "Who is she? Or at least, where did you get her?"

"May it please Your Greatness," said Pavlovich, stepping forward, "I have also captured Stephen Germain's wife. I brought her to you as soon as I thought you would have a spare moment to consider her case, as I knew you would be especially interested."

The Dictator looked speculatively at the girl's disheveled state and the bruises on her bare arms. He cocked one eye at

Pavlovich but did not express what he was thinking.

"Are you Mrs. Stephen Germain?" he asked, politely. Nicholas showed the Santa Cruz garrison for the first time that his eyes could reveal other things than their habitual iciness. A blasé charm momentarily illuminated his features.

Lillian had been somewhat astonished by the sight of the Dictator, but the way things were going she reasoned that anything could happen. She nodded her head to his question, but she said nothing.

"What are you doing here?" asked Nicholas, idly stirring his coffee.

"I am a nurse," she answered.

"Ah...I see. So you volunteered to come with the commandos to Santa Cruz, no doubt hoping to find your husband."

Lillian searched the Dictator's now implacable features, wondering just what he was getting at.

"Well, you may be pleased to know that your husband is here, my dear," he said, watching her closely.

Lillian's head bobbed to attention. She took a step forward, a world of wonderment shining through the hopelessness in her eyes. "He is!" she exclaimed. "Oh please, please let me see him! Where is he? Is he all right?"

Nicholas smiled, enjoying himself immensely. "Oh yes," he answered. "Please be assured. He must merely undergo a slight—ah—operation. On the brain, I believe it was, isn't that right, Pavlovich?"

"Yes, sir," Pavlovich grinned back, in an ecstasy of well being and self-esteem. "Just a brain operation, that's all."

Lillian looked back and forth between the two and around at all the grinning, unfriendly faces. "What is the matter with him?" she asked. "Has he been injured?"

"Oh no," said Nicholas. "But you see, after Dr. Borg has changed his brain around a little bit he will be of much greater use to us," he concluded.

"Dr. Borg!" exclaimed Lillian, horrified. "You mean—"

"Yes, my dear," sneered Nicholas. "Your precious, worldly wise news correspondent who knew how to slander the dictator of the world so well is going to be the subject of a great experiment. You should be honored. His name will go down in history as one of our most famous—*guinea pigs."*

Lillian sank to the ground. She sobbed uncontrollably, head buried in her arms and beneath the copiousness of her dark hair.

"Take her," said Nicholas, "to my quarters. I wish to question her further." He kept a straight face, but there were others who smiled knowingly. Pavlovich did not smile...

"SLIM" KENT found his guard to be in a talkative mood, on the braggadocio side.

"From this experimental station will come the supermen of a super race," he said, in fair English. "Dr. Borg's energy serum is only a war weapon. He has accomplished much greater things."

"For instance?" Kent queried, raising dull, hopeless eyes from the floor of his prison cell.

"Well, take the mother farms, for example."

Kent had heard all about the mother farms, where fanatic Russian girls, as well as female prisoners, were used for breeding purposes in order to keep up the population for future expansion.

"That's nothing new," he said. "The Nazis did it before you were born."

"But you haven't heard of Borg's cosmic conditioner rays which cause an eighty-five percent occurrence of twins and triplets. Last week one wench had quintuplets!"

Kent recoiled at the horror of it. "Dogs is a good epithet," he retorted. "So humans come in litters now."

The guard sneered. "You fathead Americans," he said. "Your race mentality has been distorted by blind adherence to your useless democratic traditions. You are incapable of adjusting yourselves to the world of Tomorrow. You have failed."

Kent looked at the guard, bored. "What about these brain experiments I've been hearing about?"

"What? You mean the experiments in surgical mutation?"

"Surgical what?"

"They haven't told us much about that, but all I gather is that Borg thinks he can make a superman by altering his brain and supercharging it. So far, his victims have turned out dead or duds. Anyway, rest assured that the end result will be another successful contribution to our cause…"

Kent spat out his unlighted cigarette onto the floor. He was particularly bitter over the fact that the second wave of the raid had been beaten off. So badly, in fact, that the third wave had not even made an appearance.

An agony of thought gripped him when he considered the possibility of Lillian's fate. And Germain! Kent never knew in his life that the dregs of misery could be so bitter. It was like physical torture. But what could he do?

DR. BORG'S underground hospital looked like a showroom at a surgical convention. White uniformed attendants entered it and left it on silent feet, as quietly efficient as automatons. They were the most experienced nurses the world could provide. Instead of interns, Borg had leading surgeons and biological technicians as his aides. They were the only ones who could have understood enough of his highly advanced work to be of any real assistance.

"All my life," the doctor was saying to Germain, the following night after the raid, while the latter lay strapped to an operating table, "I have been fascinated by the human brain, itself. I have studied it minutely in almost all species of animals as well as in man. I understand its evolution perhaps better than any other living specialist."

Borg paused, while his rubber gloves fondled a sharp, bone-cutting instrument. He snarled happily, and his left eye twitched down to half the size of the other. "I can tell you," he said, "that the human brain has, comparatively speaking, only begun to evolve. Our thinking processes are carried out through the surface convolutions, somewhat in the manner that a static electric charge clings only to surfaces, but no thinking goes on in the inner, so-called gray matter. It has been said that we use only one tenth of our brains with which to think, but I can label that contention as a gross overstatement. The percentage of the unused gray matter to the actually functioning surface convolutions represents an incalculable increase. Why? Because it is packed solid with unused cells, which in future eons will unfold like a sea anemone, developing new blood channels which will feed and activate all areas, permitting new patterns of thought to form, leaving the field wide open for the development for an endless variety of new mental faculties. We are already different from dogs, because we have a sense of color and a sense of aesthetics. Who knows of what other faculties there may be in a mere embryonic stage within the brain?

"But my experiment with you will be on a purely empirical basis rather than on a hypothetical one," he continued congenially. "I intend to speed up the process or rather the results of evolution in your brain in various ways, which I shall explain. It is very interesting."

"Yes, isn't it," said Germain. "So very charming of you."

From the looks of things, the operation was about to begin. A huge surgical machine with a battery of microscopes hung ponderously above his head, ready to be lowered over him. He saw electrical cables, small spotlights, oxygen tubes, gas tubes for anaesthetizing. Grave countenanced attendant doctors were putting on white masks. Germain's beaten mind thought sickeningly of Lillian. He felt, physically, as though his heart had broken. Life seemed to be a festering corpse. *Let them do it,* he thought, *I hope to God they kill me.*

"Superior brains," the doctor prattled on, "are merely the result of a fortunate combination of circumstances. Excellent blood delivery to the brain, a good heart, a fine endocrine system, these are the basic essentials. You have a fine endocrine system, even including the thymus. You also have a beautiful adrenaline output when required, and a high quality pituitary. The only real requisite lacking for the ordinary type of superiority is better blood delivery." He waved his hand at a glass cage beside the table. "See those plastic arteries and veins?" he said. "They are going into your head—deep in—to feed and supercharge the inner gray matter. But this is not all. I am going to open up new layers in your brain, open fields for the development of tens of thousands of new convolutions. Theoretically, in a short space of time your mentality could be equivalent, in psychic power if not in knowledge, to that of a man as he might reasonably evolve a million years from our present era."

"Tell me one thing," said Germain quietly, his somewhat battered Indian's face staring at Borg out of black, inscrutable eyes like those of an ancient tribal chieftain caught in the enemy's camp and about to be put to the test of torture. "What if I do turn out to be a superman? Then what?"

"Aha!" gleamed Borg. "Then we are only ready to begin. I shall have controls over you whereby, you will be forced to think for me. Much deep and concentrated thinking is going to be required by us, and your brain may turn out to be the very psychic instrument that can do it and arrive at the conclusions which we desire. You are about to become very valuable to the New World State. No, I amend that statement—" Borg's ugly countenance darkened before a vision of fear. He gazed beyond Germain at something conjured up by the mind, something that was unimaginably grim and terrifying, something that an advanced mind such as his could only contemplate with stern foreboding. "You are about to become a door of escape for a few individuals. Your own brain is the only road we'll have."

He glared at Germain purposefully. "That road," he said, with a snarl, "must be very, carefully constructed, but with haste."

The huge machine above Germain came down toward his head like the underside of a freight elevator. Expert hands fastened a gas mask to his face. He felt the gas surge into his lungs. There was no smell to it like the old-fashioned ether. His head swam.

Curiously, he began to count the stubby whiskers on Dr. Borg's chin as the attendant prepared his surgeon's mask. One, two, three...four...five...

The intervals between numbers had become longer and longer until now...

CHAPTER FIVE
Infant God

DARKNESS…
Soft, sweeping endlessness…
Black, infinite nebulae billowing…
In the abyss of eons a brittle ringing…
stephen germain!
Stephen Germain!
STEPHEN GERMAIN!

That's who *he* was. Ego evolving out of space. The vibration of existence commences. Life's pendulum swings. The living clock ticks. A heart without body, pulsing, pulsing, pulsing, whirling in space, gathering momentum, gaining mass, enhaloed by wobbling planets of blood. *Thrump. Thrump! THRUMP!*

Wind rushing. Velocity beyond comprehension. Faster…faster…faster! Bursting the confines of Infinity. A blast of light… Consciousness…

HE LAY in darkness, his bandaged head braced up, still on the operating table. Nearby, a nurse sat dozing.

Germain lay still and analyzed himself. Still alive, he mused. Not much damage. He felt vaguely sluggish, but he reasoned that was to be expected of a convalescent.

Then he heard his pulse beating in his temples. His heart seemed to be working at a normal rate, but with a heavier, more purposeful beat. He heard then faintly the ghastly sound of blood gurgling in plastic veins and arteries—inside his head. He suddenly felt dizzy and nauseated, and he groaned.

In an instant, the nurse was helping him. "Don't move your head," she said. "You must stay like this for some time."

After a while, Germain slept. The next day, Dr. Borg came in to see him.

"You will not notice anything unusual right away," he said, "but soon, I am sure, you will become aware of strange new things which most men have never sensed before."

Germain asked about Kent and Lillian but got no reply. So he only lay there on the operating table and thought and slept.

Once when he awoke he experienced a new sensation. It was like having a pair of eyes for the first time and seeing indescribable things like color. Among his own thoughts he *sensed* the thoughts of others. Words spoken in Russian were understandable in terms of basic ideas. He did not open his eyes.

"You going to town tonight?" one voice, speaking aloud, said to the other, in Russian. Then the same personality who had spoken *thought:* He better say no. Otherwise it means he can pay me the five hundred Bolivianos he owes me...

The person whom he addressed was thinking: I can't tell him I'm going or he'll know I've got dough. I'll pay the old tightwad next week. I can't disappoint that gorgeous, satin-looking little Latin of mine by showing up without any folding money. "No," this second one said aloud. "I've got some work to do for the sergeant." And again he thought: Nice work if you can get it! Oh boy! I can just see her now! And when I take her home—

There followed, in a few seconds of time, a vivid mental portrayal of a time-worn combination of amorous proceedings, some of them of an intimacy which a man would never share with anyone—thoughts which always remain in the individual's own mental cellar and are never voiced.

Hmmm. So it begins, thought Germain. Now I can read people's thoughts. So what?

Suddenly, his eyes opened. A startling thought occurred to him. If he could read enough thoughts around there, he might be able to find out what happened to Lillian and Kent.

Craftily, like a thief who has just made an unexpected haul, he closed his eyes and concentrated on his newfound gift. By some practice and effort he discovered that he could submerge his own conscious thoughts until their interference was negligible. When in this state, he received extraneous thoughts with amplified clarity.

After several hours of trying, he found that he could "tune in" on one series of thoughts and shield out others. At first the whole thing was as unwieldy as trying to wiggle one's ears or control other involuntary muscles, but after a while he became more skilled at it. He began to identify personalities outside the laboratory whom he had never seen.

But he was still weak from the operation. He could not do this for long without falling into an exhausted sleep.

Once, when he was awake, Dr. Borg came in and made many tests on him. He attached to his temples and the base of his brain a brain wave pattern indicating apparatus. * For long minutes he watched the visible wave patterns flow across the viewing screen, studying them carefully, as well as their reaction to various stimuli. During these tests, Germain learned how to bring his conscious thought practically to rest. He did not know, however, that this gave his wave-pattern the characteristics of a sleeping man under anaesthetic and that Dr. Borg easily detected the subterfuge in view of the fact that the patient lay awake looking at him. The old wizard realized at once that Germain's brain was growing rapidly in dexterity.

*Such apparatus is used today in various hospitals to determine epileptic cases and to identify other types characterized by visible brain wave patterns. One experiment showed visibly on a screen the subject's mental wave pattern in response to the smell of violets! —Author.

One time Germain read Borg's thought: I think I'll jab my knife through his left arm and watch the wave pattern...

When Germain turned his eyes apprehensively to look for the knife, Borg laughed. "So you *do* read minds. I knew, of course, that you were attempting to conceal your growing abilities." All the while he was watching new, powerful and complex wave patterns leap on the visual screen. Such waves he had never seen before occurring in the brain of any mortal man. "Magnificent... What a brain!" he exclaimed. "Now I see your true growth. It is remarkable."

He snarled happily, baring purplish gums. He waved a bony finger at Germain. "Just don't get too clever with that brain of yours, Mr. Stephen Germain. There are a great many things in this wide, black world that you don't know about, but I do!"

GERMAIN'S mind reached up to delve into the doctor's mind, to see what it was that made him so mysterious. For one brief moment he seemed to grasp a mass of monstrous mental impressions too incomprehensible and terrible to fathom in one instant. They were like grotesque phantoms caught at a ghoulish picnic by a lightning bolt. They, scattered before his probing mind in an infinitesimal part of a second, scurrying, it seemed, underground, and he chased them deliberately through what appeared to be catacombs, but they closed ponderous doors against him. He felt he could have burst these mental barriers asunder, but he *knew* somehow that if he did Dr. Borg would know also of his true powers, because those mental doors were deliberate barriers placed there consciously by the doctor, and Germain did not feel it prudent to let the other become aware of his soaring mental strength. However, he gathered two vague but ponderous impressions: what Borg feared was a source of terror to Nicholas the First, and the object of their mutual fear constituted a colossal threat to Humanity.

Borg now deliberately thought at him: I am something of a mentalist, myself. At least I can screen my thoughts from your exploring psycho-electric perception. Don't be too confident, young man. Remember that I can always control you. Your mind is just a toddler in a big new world never known to you before. I warn you. Unknown dangers and, yes, unknown and fiendish beings are there in that mental world to do you mortal harm if you do not do as I order you to, now I want you to relax, to rest. Close your eyes and close your mind. Relax every muscle of your body. You are drifting in peaceful darkness. You are descending into a deep well of peace and silence, where you are to sleep and rest and heal. You can do nothing else than to obey my thought, for it is your only protection, your only attachment to existence. My mental voice, Stephen Germain. To this and this alone will you respond...

Only half-hypnotized, Germain's formidable mind allowed him to fall into an exhausted sleep.

THIS TIME, when he woke up, he found himself in a new location. He was lying on a hospital bed, his head braced immovably in a special kind of stand. He was in a small, electrically lighted cell. There was one door, which was heavy and locked.

So they are afraid of me, he thought. He closed his eyes and tried to contact somebody's mind. He had never quite gotten around to testing his range.

Suddenly, he had a new experience. This time he seemed to follow a stream of thought to its source. He suddenly felt as though he were *inside* someone else. He gasped aloud. The impression faded, momentarily, and then returned, clearer than before. *He was seeing!* Seeing through someone else's eyes. He saw a corridor. Several Russian soldiers walked by the person whose eyes he was using.

My lord!—he thought. If I can do this I can find Kent. I can find Lillian—even see her. Maybe—maybe I could even *fight back!* This is it! They've given me a weapon and they don't know it. My body can lie here and I can be outside, actually. But first I must learn to control another person's will. I know it can be done now. Just got to keep plugging. Heaven help me…

CHAPTER SIX
Rescue

ONE WEEK later, an American patrol plane droned through the stratosphere near Guayaramerin. Big, telescopic night glasses were trained on the northernmost Russian outpost in the Bolivian *Beni*.

"It's a damn shame," the pilot was saying through the telephone to the observer, "that the big Santa Cruz raid failed. Helluva lot of fine commandos lost there, not to mention ships and equipment. Damn, can't we do anything to whip these dirty swine?"

"Wonder what happened to the guys that got caught," commented the observer.

Shall I tell you?

"Yeah, but how do you know?" asked the observer.

"What are you talking about?" said the pilot.

"You just said you'd tell me."

"Tell you what?"

About what happened to those who were taken prisoner.

This time, both men were aware of the thoughts of a third person. The pilot looked suspiciously at his co-pilot.

"Did you say that?" he asked.

The co-pilot had been looking dreamily away at the vast, round edge of the world and the dim stars that shone in the stratosphere even in the daytime. He awoke with a start.

"Huh? Who said what?"

"No, I guess it wasn't you. Hey, Sam!" he called to the navigator. "Were you talking on the phone just then?"

"Naw, I was shootin' a couple of stars I know. Just got Betelgeezer in the belly."

"Hank!" called the frantic pilot to the communications officer. "Were you talking on the phone?"

"Quiet," came the other's voice. "I'm receiving a time

check."

The pilot and his observer, though they could not see each other, felt the common bond of mystification draw them invisibly together.

It may seem amazing to you, but you fellows will have to believe what I am going to tell you...

"Yipe! Hey! Did you hear that?" shouted the pilot.

"Hear what?" said the co-pilot. "What is this, anyway?"

"Yes, I heard it," cried the observer.

"What in hell do you make out of it? It isn't a voice, it's *thoughts.*"

"Jeez," exclaimed the pilot. "Maybe it's true they talk to you up here." His face was covered with cold perspiration.

"Say, you feel all right?" queried the co-pilot. "You look pale as a hermit crab's belly. You cold or something? Look at the goose pimples on your hands. An' you're sweatin'! I got it. We never shoulda drunk that pre-war stuff we picked up in Iquitos."

The pilot swallowed hard. His complexion had just the suggestion of a delicate pastel green in it. "I tell you there's a guy talkin' to me," he insisted. "An' he isn't on board this ship..."

"Aw, you're gettin' batty. Maybe you better—"

The pilot waved his hand for silence. His eyes went wide, staring into space. "Listen," he hissed.

My name is Stephen Germain. I will not take time to tell you in detail how I accomplish this mental telepathy or how it is that I can see your plane and read your minds. The object of my contacting you is to arrange a rescue...

"Hey!" shouted the co-pilot to the other members of the crew. "Mack has passed out or something. He's in a trance!"

"So is Ernie," called the navigator, referring to the observer. "He's just staring blank into space. What's goin' on around here?"

SIX HOURS later, at Lima base, an irate general was stomping back and forth in front of two wild-eyed airmen and a roomful of variously skeptical and openmouthed lesser officials of the Sixth Airforce Command and the Strategic Services Division.

"But it cannot be true," he snorted, while all his medals jangled discordantly. He slapped the bald spot on his head in desperation. "Yet, the information you have given concerning Captain Germain and Major Kent and the Santa Cruz base could not have been known by you two," he waved his hands in a gesture of despair, appealing to the chief representative of Strategic Services. "What do you make of it?"

The middle-aged colonel from Strategic Services looked like nobody's fool. But besides being a realist he also had imagination. He was a tall, thin man with a black mustache and *pince-nez*, a bald head and a distinguishing scar across his forehead. When he spoke, it was with slow deliberation. The pilot and the observer who had heard voices in the stratosphere looked at him hopefully.

"We have gathered, so far, the following facts," he said. "These two men, according to their companions, were flying in the stratosphere above Guayaramerin when they fell into a species of trance. They remained in that condition for one half-hour. During that time, so they say, they were addressed at length, telepathically, by our own operative, Captain Stephen Germain. He told them about the Santa Cruz raid and his part in it. He told them about Major Kent's imprisonment, in addition to a heretofore-unknown fact that we have only been able to verify partially, that is, that Nicholas the First is in Santa Cruz. Also, he described to them the plight of his wife, Lieutenant Lillian Germain, who is now in the Dictator's personal custody.

"Furthermore, he outlined to them a very strange plan,

whereby Major Kent, Lieutenant Germain and a few others of the imprisoned survivors might escape. He made mention of mental powers, which rapidly acquire new proportions each day, due to some experiment of Dr. Borg's to which he was subjected, and he claims that he now feels in a position to put guards to sleep, dominate wills and, in short, completely fix the camp so that a small rescue party might get in unharmed, pick up survivors, and get out safely again."

"Yes, yes, of course," said the general in command of the Sixth Airforce. "We know all that, but what do you *think* of it?"

"We cannot believe everything we hear without some sort of proof," answered the colonel, unperturbedly. "Still, we have been given some startling facts already, which could not have been known to these two airmen."

"How do we know it's not some new trick of that mad Russian, Dr. Borg?" asked the general. "We already know about brain wave emanations. We can measure and amplify them. Maybe he's found a way of putting his thoughts on the air, I don't know. I've read the story of that fellow's life in pre-war days and we also have your own more official data on him and you know as well as I that bio-chemistry is not his only field. He has distinguished himself in about ten major fields of science and is also one of those Svengali mystic types, I wouldn't put anything past him. We can't take any more chances."

"It is not too difficult," said the colonel, "to arrive at conclusive facts. It is reasonable to assume that if Captain Germain actually communicated with these two airmen he would no doubt be concerned enough about the outcome to follow events in his mind. I therefore suggest that the two men who first received these impressions return to the same location and attempt to make a new contact with Germain, I, myself, will go along. I know some personal data concerning

Germain that only he would be able to tell me. I shall ask him concerning these things, either mentally, or through one of these two airmen. If we can thus positively prove that it is Germain who is sending the thought messages, then I suggest—"

The general stared at the colonel. Suddenly, he struck the palm of his hand with his fist. "Congratulations!" he said. "That's good common sense right smack in the middle of a nightmare. We'll do it and see what happens. And if this turns out to be valid, I'll send a large enough ship to pick up any and all survivors. I'll send three volunteers in a strato-transport and cover them with two dozen fighters to hang around upstairs just in case—"

NICHOLAS THE FIRST had decided to prolong his stay in Santa Cruz. It was a good point of vantage from which to direct the Grand Attack that was designed to expel all democratic forces from Latin America. Vast sky trains and huge submarine freighters were bringing supplies daily to Argentina, Uruguay, Paraguay, Bolivia and Chile, out of busy Eurasian factories. Great attack fleets were now almost complete. Secret reports on the Asiatic fleets were also very gratifying to Nicholas. He felt his heel well planted on the neck of the surface world. If the enemy should pull new tricks out of the bag in their last moment of desperation, Nicholas had such an overwhelming reserve trick up his sleeve that he was afraid of it, himself—even sorry that he had tinkered with it. He, the man who took no chances, had ended up by taking the greatest chance of any of Earth's rulers before him. This thing was far worse than the atomic bomb. It was more like the threat of a true chain reaction. It might prove to be a terrible boomerang that could, in the moment of his highest triumph, utterly destroy him.

He and Dr. Borg, two of his highest aides, and one very

special personal advisor, were the only ones who were aware of this super blitz weapon that he held in reserve. The special advisor, Svenga, was even at that moment engaged in a secret mission to a certain mysterious country for the purpose of guaranteeing the docility of the weapon, through the medium of diplomatic prostration and impossible promises of reward. The weapon was a treaty backed by some rather wolf-sized teeth—on the side of the "weapon." It was, as Dr. Borg had so aptly pointed out, a pact with the real and living Hell, itself…

"LILLIAN," said Nicholas, as he sat back in his chair and munched slowly on some giant Concepción peanuts, "this asinine American individual initiative is especially unbecoming in a woman, I think you would be a positively irresistible female if you were less independent."

Lillian Germain sat expressionlessly, except for an impression of coldness, in another chair, hardly hearing what was said. She was dressed in fairly becoming clothes which had been brought in from Buenos Aires, flown to Santa Cruz in compliance with the Dictator's request. She herself, unable to resist her passion for flowers in the midst of the tropics, had almost subconsciously fashioned a casual corsage of angel's trumpet with a sprig of red Bougainville to her blouse. Nicholas had ordered her a complete makeup and she found herself fit, at least in appearance, to step out onto the streets of any metropolis. But she did not appear to care or even to notice. Her blue-green eyes gazed listlessly into space. Her full red lower lip was pursed out more than usual.

Her mind was on Germain and Kent. She had heard nothing nor any sign of life from either of them since first meeting the Dictator, except for one thing. They did tell her that her husband had survived the operation and that he was alive and well. At least that was something, she thought.

Still, if he had been reported dead, she would have had only herself to think of, which she would have considered a negligible matter. But with him still alive somewhere in this nightmarish camp it gave her food for tortured thought. What had they done to him? Imagination under such circumstances is a cruel companion, bringing to the mind the unwanted but most feared visions of horror worse than reality.

Oh Stephen, *Stephen*—she thought. If I could only find you and know that you are all right. This she repeated periodically, like an emotional pulse-beat surging out of the soul.

"You do not seem to be interested in my company," said Nicholas, suddenly glaring at her stonily. His eyes glistened with a feline intentness, as though he were studying a mouse and plotting diabolic trickery. "I think your American idea of woman suffrage is sheer, driveling idiocy and I will tell you why. In this world we must be guided by fundamental law. In regard to womankind, fundamental law says that her purpose is for reproduction, for the mothering of her offspring and the maintenance of the home. Fundamental law also says that the male is the master, the stronger, the wiser, the hunter and protector. He does the fighting and the deciding."

The Dictator was warming up to his megalomania. He leaned forward across the bowl of roasted peanuts and his unfinished correspondence of State, fixing his gaze upon Lillian, who was slowly becoming aware of the other's sharply knitted brow and his intense, penetrating stare. There was a Satanic handsomeness about him when he was this way, which fascinated her in spite of herself.

"For these reasons I abolished the equality of womanhood in Russia and in every nation which has come under my rule. Much of the old Soviet Union was not as fundamental in its doctrine as the Marxists would like historians to paint it—especially in regard to women.

"Get away from those fundamentals I mentioned and what have you? Ha! It is what you have now in America, and it is hideous. Stupid women asserting themselves in politics while other women's committees are wondering what do to about the shameful increase in divorces, the disintegration of the home, the tens of thousands of delinquent minors filling your juvenile courts, the marital incompatibility, madhouses filled to capacity, sex murders, *perversion*." Nicholas was bitterly angry now. "You women have caused all of this. But your men are groveling, vegetable weaklings." He stood up and came around his desk to where Lillian was sitting. "Do you know the fundamental answer to it all, and the beginning of all happiness? Do you?"

Lillian made a little quick motion with her head, which tossed her raven-black hair over her shoulders. It was a gesture of defiance. She looked up at him stubbornly but said nothing, although the man could see by the increased rise and fall of her breast that she was apprehensive of him. Suddenly, he pulled her roughly to her feet.

"It is this," he said. And he crushed her to him, kissing her brutally on the mouth.

WITH all her strength, she struck the side of his jaw with her fist. The blow struck hard and—because of her wedding ring that they had permitted her to keep—drew blood from an ugly cut.

Nicholas did not mind the cut. He stood there and laughed in a horrible kind of way, for through the mask of his mirth she saw his temper flaming. Suddenly the laugh was gone as though cut by a knife. Only the temper was left. His lip curled in a sneer and he struck her a blow that sent her reeling to the floor. Her mind swam in black confusion, pierced with pain. Both her nostrils ran red with blood.

He took hold of her hair and yanked her up again. "Woman!" he shouted. "Ha! Nicholas will teach your sex that fundamental happiness lies only in your blind obedience to and dependence upon man. In the World State there is no room for incompatibility and degenerate husbands, or for broken homes or child revolt against parents. It is against my laws, and it is against natural law!"

He threw her into her chair and went back to his desk. But he still had more to say. He looked at her just as intently, but the tone of his voice changed. He adopted a tone of sincerity backed by a sort of practical, fatherly sternness. "Now look here," he said, "I expect more out of you than adolescent hysterics. When I first saw you I took you for something unusual, in every way I've always desired a woman to be. I am very much interested in you, Lillian, in a personal way. You are beautiful, but I have seen the pick of beauties from thirty nations. I've had them in any type or variety, like grapes on a vine. So don't imagine for one minute that this is a case of fascination solely for your physical charms. Fortunately for you, I am perhaps a bit blasé in that respect. But there is a real, vibrant life and intellect to you, which is stimulating to me. I should like to have you as my constant companion.

"I have played rough with you because I had to, but above all you will find me to be a very reasonable man. Your husband criticized me, in his writings, because he, himself, is blind to the facts. So do not discredit me on the basis of my philosophies."

A telephone rang and an orderly dashed into the room with a message. Lillian looked battered and weary, so Nicholas desisted and returned to his affairs of state for the moment.

She lay crumpled in her chair, face buried in her arms.

With one hand she held a handkerchief to her bleeding nose. Oh Stephen, Stephen!—was all she could think, spasmodically.

Lillian, I hear you, darling. Do not betray me. Pretend not to notice anything.

The thought came unmistakably into her head from an outside source, as clear and as powerful as a great, deep-throated bell. Nicholas heard her catch her breath, but he thought, with satisfaction, that she was sobbing. "Women," he muttered, in proud disdain, and he continued reading official documents.

Oh Lord—she thought, shaking with an uncontrollable excitement. Do not torture me with such dreams.

But do not be tortured, Lillian, came the powerful, overwhelming thought again. *If you will remain calm and quiet I shall prove to you it is I who am sending you my thoughts, and no one else. Remember our secret album in the little brown trunk in your mother's attic in Westwood? It is our honeymoon album that nobody has seen but you and me. The best picture of all is the one we had taken by that old one-legged fisherman on the pier at Catalina. You were laughing in that picture and handing me a coke bottle, and I was holding a hotdog in each hand. Remember our wedding night? When I held your priceless body in my arms there in the little honeymoon cabin at Avalon and told you of a great dream I had, of how I wanted to enter into world politics and fight all my life for Man's enlightenment, to help set the world back on its feet again? Remember that hill overlooking Culver City that we called our penthouse and all those nights we spent parked in my old Studebaker, and the time when I—*

Oh Stephen! My darling!—she thought back, blindly, unquestioningly, in spite of the incomprehensible miracle it seemed he was performing. She bit her handkerchief into shreds and sobbed audibly. They killed you!—she thought.

Poor darling. I can't tell you to be calm, but I can tell you that I am not dead. I am very well, in fact much better than you think. Borg may not know it, but he has given me a powerful weapon of defense. I dare not reveal my real strength until I am ready, because it is still in his power to kill me. So do not let on to anyone that I am communicating with you. I have had you under observation for days, but now things are coming to a head where I have to let you know certain plans. But I have to work carefully. Borg is very clever. He has many powers of his own. And I have sensed many other things too vast and terrible for your comprehension. The main thing is to get you and Kent out of here. Now you just lie still and listen to my plan.

But, Steve, sweetheart—she thought back—please tell me what Borg did to you. Where are you? How are you, really? She even thought, involuntarily: What are you?

I must confess, came Germain's powerful communication, *that Borg has changed me. He has completely altered my brain. He has cut my skull and installed expansion plates for brain growth. My brain has been opened like an artichoke and stuffed with synthetic arteries, veins and capillaries. He feeds me high vitamin content foods, shoots me with energy serum, transplants specialized cells into my body, which drive me half crazy with super energy. My brain is already using those expansion plates, and I feel—*

"Oh, Stephen!" she cried aloud, uncontrollably.

For heaven's sake, Lillian!

NICHOLAS looked up with a start from his papers. His eyes glared at the woman, suspiciously.

"I—I had a nightmare," she explained, lamely. She searched the Dictator's face but found it to be as unreadable as usual. She could not know what was going on in that dark mind.

Nicholas' mind is a controlled one, came Germain again, telepathing to his wife. *Just like Dr. Borg's, except not quite so strong. I can only read surface thoughts, unless I force myself through. But if I do that he will be aware of my power. Sometimes I wonder, though, just what they could do about it if I let loose and put them all to sleep. Dr. Borg has half-hypnotized me into believing that if I try my mental wings he can clip them off. Somehow I don't think he's kidding me. I have sensed something unmistakably powerful, like an alien intelligence, so powerful and menacing that Borg and Nicholas themselves are afraid of it. Terrible shadows hang over this poor old world of ours, darling. When I open up with my heavy artillery I know I am going to be in for some surprises. So all I can do is wait and plan and nurse my increasing strength. Do you know that I can see, through another man's eyes, anything I want for a radius of hundreds of miles; that I can even possess that person's body and mind and will? I can also see, in an indescribable way, without the use of another person's eyes. Not only can I see but I can feel beyond myself. I can feel the pain in your head, darling, caused by that blow Nicholas gave you. And I can short-circuit an average mind by concentrated mental energy. I killed three chickens and a pig yesterday. Just seemed to blowout a fuse in their little brains. I think today I could slay Nicholas, but I—*

Lillian was gazing wide-eyed into space, terrified.

Lillian! You fear me. No, don't, darling. Don't fear me, please. I can assure you that the highest thoughts accompany my increase in power.

The powerful blast of Germain's thoughts shut off, momentarily. *Ah, what a fool I am,* he came again. *How unwise I was to reveal to you the real truth about myself. I forgot that love is based on mutual interest and understanding. Now this incomprehensible thing I have revealed estranges you to me. It strikes at all the old racial memories and instincts of the female, at your inborn fear of the unknown, at the dark powers of the Serpent, I feel your mind shrink from its contact with me as you might draw in your skirts at the sight of a sewer rat.*

While you are still receptive to me, however, I must outline to you the plan of action I have worked out whereby you may escape…

IN LIKE MANNER, Germain sought out Kent's startled mind and revealed his plan. He told him of his contact with the American flyers. He cautioned him to secrecy, mentioning again his deep presentiment of unimaginable dangers lurking somewhere deep within the incomprehensible darkness of this new mental world into which he was slowly groping his way. He said they were dangers of which Borg and Nicholas were secretly aware, dark powers with which Nicholas had made a treaty. He told him that he, Kent, would have to escape with Lillian and some of the other survivors because the fight against the Russians and the Asiatics was only a secondary matter compared with the real hidden menace which hovered over Nicholas the First and the world like a vast, light-obliterating vampire, and that he would need Kent's help later in the United States.

I feel, he thought to Kent, *when I probe Borg's mind—as far as I dare—that I sense the evil power of Hell behind him. It may sound incredible to you, Slim, but my mind is awake to concepts to which all of the rest of you are pitiably and hopelessly blind. We are like ten sheep sleeping miraculously in the midst of ten thousand wolves, and I sense that we are about to be devoured.*

I—I don't get you, Steve—Kent thought back from his prison.

You don't have to—yet, thought Germain. *The main thing is this escape of yours.*

But what about you?

I must remain; I don't want to be seen by you or Lillian again.

What do you mean?

My brain is growing, Slim. I am a monstrosity. It means the end for Lillian and myself. You've got to take over, Kent, and God bless you. I know you've always loved her.

But, Steve. What will happen to you? Kent's mind struggled in a maelstrom of doubts and emotions, momentary vistas of undreamed of happiness blotted out, spasmodically, by stubborn loyalty.

When the rescue is pulled, I'll have to show my mental muscles, thought Germain. *When I do, there'll be a war on between me and*

Borg—and something unknown that I think he's going to call into the fight—something that you normal humans might call—supernatural.

I can't understand this, Steve—protested Kent. In his lonely cell he shook his head and wiped his perspiring brow with his one good hand.

Just be ready when I call you, answered Germain.

THAT NIGHT many strange things transpired at Santa Cruz. First, an American strato-transport began to circle gingerly above the base, in the stratosphere. The volunteer pilot was the same one who had first contacted Germain over Guayaramerin and who had subsequently communicated with him again. This night the same method of communication was employed.

Hey, Germain!—thought the pilot.

I am with you, resounded Germain's ponderous thought, miles above Zone 7. *You may descend at once and carry out the plan as discussed. Do not contact me further, as I must concentrate on other things vital to your safety.*

As the plane descended, the Radar watch at Zone 6 in Cochabamba picked it up. They questioned Zone 7 about it. Mechanically, Zone 7 watch replied, "Ship identified and passed. Special mission attached to staff of Nicholas the First."

The blacked out transport landed without incident at the Santa Cruz airport. On the field waiting for it, was a silent, wondering little huddle of American survivors of the commando raid.

The co-pilot and the navigator waited on board while they watched their pilot, somewhat nervously, as his dark figure sprinted across the field toward the approaching group of people.

"Major Kent?" asked the pilot, gun in hand, as he arrived in front of the group. "Lieutenant Germain?"

"I am Major Kent," said a man in a battle-torn uniform. He had one shriveled looking arm in a sling. "This is Lieutenant Germain." He indicated a pale-faced, silent young woman who was rather neatly dressed in civies for such an occasion. Behind her crowded two frightened nurses and five commandos. These latter were carrying the documents and serum samples they had originally come for.

"We have room for fifty people," said the pilot.

"We are the sole survivors," said Kent. "The Russians are all asleep. It is an amazing thing, what Germain is doing. The strain must be killing him. Let's get out as quickly as possible."

"Then Germain, I guess, is not—"

"No—" from Kent. "He is not coming with us."

The woman with him bent her head and emitted a piteous cry of anguish.

The little group then ran to the plane and got in. Without further incident, it took off and climbed toward the stratosphere. When it had reached the desired altitude and joined its well-armed escort of fighters, Lillian Germain heard once more from her husband.

You are momentarily free, he thought to her, this time not so powerfully. She could sense a terrible exhaustion in him. *Go and find your happiness with Slim Kent. Do not grieve for me, my darling. I have a grave struggle ahead, but I must survive it, because after that one victory I shall have to dedicate all my powers to save this world from Armageddon itself...*

That was all. Kent's arm remained around Lillian's bowed figure as they flew through the stratosphere. Their senses were too dulled by the overwhelming proportions of recent events to appreciate the glory of the almost naked stars...

CHAPTER SEVEN
Bound or Unbound?

THE MINUTE Germain released his mental grip on the Santa Cruz camp it came to life. Exhausted though he was by the ordeal, he lay alert in his locked cell and held teleperceptive guard on himself. His extra-sensory vision took in his surroundings in a circle whose diameter was roughly three hundred yards. He gave a thorough going over to each person's mind entering that area.

The first thing that happened was something that had been inspired secretly by Pavlovich. Pavlovich had been somewhat taken back, after the operation on Germain, to learn that he was still so much alive, and that he had acquired such intrinsic value in the eyes of the Dictator. He had aired his suspicions of Germain, but had been cut rather short by Nicholas. Now, however, he saw his chance.

"That's that brain of Borg's that did it," he told one of the most frightened looking guards. "Somebody's got to kill it, quick."

Pavlovich, wary enough because of what he had just seen demonstrated and what he had overheard previously from Borg, stayed well out of Germain's sphere of vigilance. The guard to whom he had spoken, however, responded in the calculated manner. Before anyone could stop him, he ran as though berserk toward that end of the subterranean hospital that housed Germain. He carried a supersonic projector.

Germain was weak, but still effective.

Before the guard could open up the death ray on his cell, the fellow's brain went dead, all its nerve dendrites singed short by an overload of psycho-electric force. He dropped lifeless to the floor. Pavlovich retired from the gathering crowd outside. He knew that if he were going to destroy Germain it would have to be by a better method. But he would find that method.

Then came Dr. Borg and Nicholas, and Golovinsky. Borg told the others to stay at the hospital entrance, to calm down, and that he, himself, would take care of the situation. Nicholas wanted to follow, but Borg motioned him back.

"This is dangerous," he said. "See that dead guard? Keep back. I'll handle this myself…"

Nicholas called after him, "Either you demonstrate you can handle him," he demanded from the door, "or I'll have him blasted out if we have to do it by long range artillery. He is too dangerous even for you to be playing with, Borg."

"Stephen Germain is about to become a useful instrument of the New World State," announced Borg grimly, as he looked at his watch and continued his limping advance down the hall. "You forget that his powers are of my creation."

Germain could have killed him, but he was startled to read in Borg's mind that the latter knew he would not be killed, for the simple reason that there were things in the doctor's mind which his patient would want to know. So Germain probed him, frantically, only to come up against those heavy mental doors again. He strained, sending a psychic battering ram at those barriers. And he broke through.

He found a second barrier wall in the form of a prepared thought for his analysis. It concerned a sleeping gas which Borg was about to admit to his chamber, so he suddenly took possession of the doctor and held him, as still as a statue. But Borg's was a difficult mind to keep down.

You think you are very clever—Borg thought at him—but you failed to extract from me the full details of the sleeping gas. Of course that is because you were afraid, before, to break through my shield and reveal your true powers. But now it is too late. That sleep gas is set to go off automatically. I had it fixed so that if its moving control was not set back by hand every hour it would automatically be discharged and put you to sleep. So we would have been released eventually from your control whether you wanted to release us or not. The sleep gas should be on right now. When you fall asleep I shall make a slave of your subconscious mind so that it may solve great problems for me, problems which are vital to myself, personally—and *not* to the New World State.

Germain already heard the gas hissing into his room. He was drowsy in spite of his gigantic will. In a last moment of desperation, he struck out at Borg.

Those watching the doctor from the doorway saw him grasp his temples in pain, saw the heavy death's head cane drop to the polished floor. He staggered.

Borg fought Germain's weakened blast but felt fire in his brain nevertheless. Then the pain subsided, gradually, and he knew that the white sleep fog was sweeping Germain irresistibly into peaceful sleep.

Immediately, he entered the chamber where Germain was lying, shutting off the gas as he did so. Then he spent one half hour with him, subjecting him to the most thorough hypnosis of which he was capable—and Borg was one of the world's most adept.

After he was sure that he was absolutely under control, he set a problem before his subconscious mind...

DAYS LATER, Dr. Borg wrote down the following in his medical diary:

The subconscious mind is merely a perfect robot mechanism. It is like a super-calculating machine. Once a certain problem has been fed into it, it builds up the possibilities with a precise logic, working constantly in spite of the condition of the conscious mind. Its only limitation is human knowledge. Still, the conscious mind of Man is not persistent enough to make every possible combination of known facts. Latent in the warehouse of Human Knowledge are answers to unnumbered great problems yet unsolved. I have caused Germain to absorb out of my own mind all that I know on the subjects of mathematics, astronomy, electro-physics and all related fields of knowledge which I believe necessary to his solving the problem of interplanetary navigation. His conscious mind will never know these things, but his subconscious mind will use them. Sooner or later, if the solution lies within range of the known facts, Germain's tremendous mentality must produce the answer.

What Borg did not consider proper material for his medical log was the further thought: Then, in the last analysis, in case of mortal danger, I might escape from *them*... As he thought this he looked about him in the empty room, guiltily, as though even his thoughts might be overheard.

Nicholas, he continued musing, was a naive fool to have Svenga prepare an official treaty for the foes of Agarthi. What if they do help us in case an American surprise weapon shows up? How can we ever be sure now that they won't turn on us anyway? Still, Svenga's uncouth "friends" will be my only recourse if Germain starts to get out of hand. The greatest mentality conceivable, if unaided by the unimaginably advanced weapons of the Elder Gods, could not outfight *that* spawn of Hell!

Then he wrote further in his log:

As long as I can use Germain I shall keep him alive and healthy. His development represents the greatest surgical triumph of modern times. The entire experiment has succeeded beyond expectations. But Germain, I know, is a high idealist. This idealism may have progressed in equal proportion with his mental faculties. If so, his psychic power makes a dangerous combination that I must watch over very closely.

He thought another moment, while his left eye twitched nervously. Then he added:

Prometheus was chained to a mountain because he gave Man the secret of fire. This time, however, the second Prometheus has been chained before he could get into any serious trouble. He will bring to Mankind only that which is convenient to the New World State...

Borg looked at a calendar in front of him. He also looked at his watch. Then he wrote:

2400. Eve of Victory. Tomorrow is A-day, and our Grand Attack begins...

AND SO it did. The Russians plowed northward on two widely separated fronts. One front swept downward out of Puno and Cuzco, from the Lake Titicaca region. Here twelve armored divisions thundered down like an avalanche upon the American and Peruvian positions. The attack had been preceded by three hours of rocket barrages, which cleaned a path through steel fortifications and Incan ruins alike. Already the western air armada, consisting of five thousand strato-bombers, was plastering all strategic points in western South America that lay north of their own lines. The food and equipment factories of Arequipa, the arsenals, airfields and communications centers at Lima, Limatambo and Las Palmas, the docks at Callao, the navy hydroplane base at Ancon, even the great and lofty workings of the Cerro de Pasco mines were plastered. The hydroelectric plants and steel mills of Chimbote and the Santa Valley and the copper flotation plants at Samne, and the mines at Quiruvilca, all were reduced to useless rubble. The oilfields at Talara and Negritos were blasted out of the ground, even the paper and sugar mills at Paramonga.

In Ecuador, half of Guayaquil became river bottom. The mountain fortress of Quito was left in smoking ruins, like a dying volcano, as was proud Bogota, capital of Colombia, while Cali and Medillin and the whole great Cauca Valley was razed to ruin.

On the east coast the picture was the same. Porto Alegre, Curityba, the great industrial city of Sao Paulo, scenic and strategic Rio de Janeiro, Recife, Belem do Pará, as well as Cayenne, Parimaribo, and Georgetown—all were cast under the shadow of a second strato-bomber fleet of five thousand ships. Out of Uruguay into Brazil rolled fifteen armored divisions across a smoldering highway prepared by rocket bombardment.

But this was not all by far. In the skies of Panama, Costa Rica, Nicaragua, Salvador, Guatemala, British Honduras and Mexico, appeared the astounding Asiatic fleet—fully twenty thousand strong. Long range super bombers from vast hidden factories in Burma, China, Mongolia and Siberia. While their ally in the south ground northward, the Asiatics plowed methodically through Central American skies all day—and all the next night, bombing without respite. When they began to force their landings the next day, three hundred thousand parachutes whitened the skies: tanks, rocket-launching equipment, supersonic apparatus and provisions followed.

On all fronts the Americans, Canadians, British, Australians and all their Latin American allies fought back with all they had. Hand to hand, bayonet to bayonet, machine bullet for machine bullet, rocket for rocket, ray for ray, flame for flame, tank for tank, bomb for bomb—and man for man. But mathematics favored the Russo-Asiatic hordes. Numbers. Superiority in numbers and equipment, the result of a generation of inhumanly cold planning on the part of half an enemy world.

In Chicago, seat of the U. S. Government, the president and his cabinet members lost weight and confidence. Grave men of state with years of experience behind them could see the inevitable writing on the wall. To hold South America would be to weaken their main line reserves so much that they would be inadequate for a last ditch stand on the home front. The armed forces of the Democratic Nations would have to retreat, as best they could, before they were completely routed.

On the home front the shadow of defeat stretched out its hand and the people of the nation began to lose faith in a tradition—the old, old tradition of, "It can't happen here!" After working hours they walked in the streets and stared at each other. The old mirage of "Better days inevitably around the corner" had faded in a gathering cyclone. The end of individual liberty was close, and there was apparently nothing that could be done.

"Use the *bomb!*" cried the papers.

"Suicide is better than slavery!" cried other headlines.

The whole world knew that every fighting nation had atomic bombs. Fear of gruesome retaliation kept the *bomb* in many an arsenal cellar. Chicago stated with an air of official hopelessness that the *bomb* was out of the question. It was too late.

"Too late with too little! Too late with too little!" cried mobsters, marching on the capital. The mobsters should have been working in defense plants. The militia called out to fend them off should have been fighting the enemy.

America, light of freedom, was crumbling. The churches filled with men and women who pounded their breasts and cried out to God for liberation. For who else could help them now?

FAR AWAY below the belly of the world, in a dark cell beneath a Bolivian jungle, that one other entity lay sleeping. For weeks a super-vitalized heart had pumped rich new blood into a thousand new regions of his brain. For weeks new endocrine substances had been building up the cell structure, thus bringing about an ever more powerful generation of psycho-electric forces. So powerful had this mind become, so intricate and versatile was it, that it could not lie dormant under any condition. Even from the smothering blanket of hypnotic sleep, a segment of consciousness had to emerge. And this deliberately fought to release the remainder...

I am a shapeless thing, an ego drifting down the abyss of reasonlessness. Where is my destination? What is the fundamental purpose that gives me being? What is the tenuous barrier between me and nothingness? Why do I exist? Whither must I go? Let me be form and shape, let me dimensionalize. Location, length, breadth, depth, duration. Somewhere in space and time I have a physical anchorage. Where is my body?

Dim perception of the skull's brittle envelope. Blood gurgling in synthetic arteries. In the depths of being, a heart *thrumping* mightily, like a pendulum beating the measure of existence.

I am lonely. I am a monstrosity buried in a tomb. No! I am a mortal man and I love a woman! Lillian! Lillian, my darling!

Sphere of inner perception racing outward, seeing without vision, seeing by knowing, incomprehensible awareness— expanding through space itself, to northern latitudes. *Lillian.* Lillian, my lost wife!

LILLIAN GERMAIN could not open her eyes. She lay in bed in her darkened bedchamber, motionless, relaxed. Her mind was elsewhere. Some monstrous thing, unseeable, unknowable, had found her finite mind and plucked it from its shell like some rare pearl, to dance into endlessness.

Lillian, I am lonely. I am as one buried alive without you. I need you for my own existence. Come with me across the endlessness of thought to a thousand worlds that I shall make for you out of the nothingness, just as real as the old one we have known, for it, too, evolved from the nothingness. Share knowledge of life and death. Do not fight me with fear, my dearest one. Come to me, bride of my thought.

I cannot support in solitude the magnitude of a mind that encompasses the world. I must have you with me. I shall die without you!

I am a mere woman—she replied, as though defending herself in a dream. You betray yourself to think that one such as I could be companion to a god. Leave me to my mortal ways, Stephen, my lost love and beloved husband, if you have ever loved me. But because I shall always love the memory of you as you were I must tell you this. Match your mind with a problem that will challenge it. Do you not see your road, dearest one? It is the world, the once bright world you talked so much about. You were no nationalist; you were a dreamer of universal security and enduring happiness for all Mankind. Now you hover like a god above the Earth and yet you occupy yourself with one insignificant mortal being rather than seek to save us all from slavery. Put that mighty shoulder to the wheel, O my Prometheus, and if you ever once loved this simple mortal, if you ever carried the torch of altruism, *fight!*—as only you may discover that you can...

Lillian awoke with a start, eyes wide with a terror of the great Unknown. Something had suddenly released her from a nightmare that seemed unfathomable. She trembled uncontrollably, reaching for her robe and turning on the light beside her bed. She had an inexplicable sense of immensity surrounding her, which made her so infinitesimally small that she felt lost.

But that dreaded feeling about the war and defeat was gone. The lost tradition of confidence was being replaced by a new faith in something that she could not even describe. However, she knew that it was nothing fictitious. It was real...

CHAPTER EIGHT
Foes of Agarthi

NICHOLAS the First had been served the sweetest fruits of victory. In four months, South America was his. His forces and those of his Asiatic allies were in good enough condition to stage the final attack on the United States within two months. Congratulations heaped upon him from New Moscow and urgent appeals were sent for his return to the capital of the New World State.

But Nicholas was gravely worried. He sent for Borg.

"You've fooled around enough with that freak brain of Stephen Germain's," he said, peremptorily. "Now I want you to destroy it."

Borg snarled and scowled at the same time. "Why do you want to kill the goose that is laying the golden egg?" he said.

Nicholas' eyes were not so piercing any more. They were bloodshot with sleeplessness and he only glared dully back at the doctor as he answered. "Germain is taking too long to figure out what we want, and in the meantime he grows freakishly powerful and menacing. Why his powers are equal to one of those ancient ro machines Svenga describes, which can make anyone do as the operator wishes. He is fully as much a danger to us as the foes of Agarthi. I've made one mistake, but I won't make it twice. You must destroy him."

"Ah, but Nicholas, if you only knew the progress I have made with his subconscious mind. I swear it will not be long before I shall have from it the secret we both desire. Then we can destroy him."

Nicholas looked up at Borg with one raised eyebrow. *"Can* you destroy him?"

Borg hesitated for a brief moment. Then he said, "Yes, there is a means within my knowledge of destroying him— when I wish it."

"I wish to God I could share your confidence," snapped the other, distractedly referring to a deity whom his philosophy excluded.

"But it's true," said Borg. "And furthermore—"

"I suspect," interrupted Nicholas, "that you rather cherish Germain's brain, like Gipetto who made Pinocchio and thought he was a father. Well, I may be moved to have that dangerous toy of yours destroyed unless results are produced immediately."

"Gravitation," said Borg, *"is the resistance of matter to the passage of negatively charged cosmic particles."*

"Where did that come from? The brain?"

"Yes, from Germain," said Borg, his queer eyes gleaming. "This points the way. It means that gravitation may be neutralized by some kind of force field which would so align the atoms as *not* to offer resistance, but rather, mutual attraction."

"And I suppose Germain can solve that?"

"He can. He is already doing it. His brain is a miraculous machine. Under hypnosis he has sat at a drawing board and laid out electrical and radiotronic diagrams based on new mathematics that evolves within his brain. He visualizes complicated wirings with hundreds of times the mental tenacity of a world champion chess player. Then he sketches from subconscious memory. I'll have soon some interesting completed diagrams necessary for creating the machinery that can generate a neutralizing field. You might call our objective 'degravity plates.' When we have these, all the rest is easy— air, food, heat, light, equipment. Your factories could build a ship in a month."

A flash of hope lighted Nicholas' tired eyes. "If this is really valid," he said, "then I would have an extra ace up my sleeve, even against *them*—the foes of Agarthi. Just think, Borg, if, we could really do it... Why, perhaps I could find a new ally on another world and return with some of the ancient weapons myself, to really conquer this worm-eaten world!"

Borg saw in the Dictator's eyes such fires as only a madman's dreams can nourish.

"If you can speak out into space through their guard rays, maybe," said the doctor. "You know that extra-terrestrial beings have tried to land here before and were wiped out, according to Svenga. The deros don't want surface people to advance into higher science.

"But let's not discuss this further. You'd better cut it out of your mind. I know we may be far removed from them, but *they* can read our thoughts even here. As a matter of fact I think they must have certain representatives in the Andean caverns running through Ecuador, Peru and Chile. They could be as close to us as La Paz.

"Now I must confess something to you concerning Germain. He *is* getting out of my own power to keep him controlled, yet I must keep him healthy and supercharged if he is to help us soon enough. We need him, but without help from other sources I, myself, would perhaps be powerless to resist him if he ever once got an opportunity to short out my dendrites—that is, kill me by a blast of psycho-electric energy, of which he has plenty. His seething brain is a powerful battery and a psychic force transmitter."

"But you said you could destroy him..."

"Yes," said Borg, enigmatically. "With certain assistance."

"Meaning?"

"I have a plan. Let us allow them to make him obedient."

"*No!*" Nicholas' brows raised in astonished protest.

"Yes. It would allay their suspicions for us to let them in on this thing. We'll present the thing as though we considered Germain dangerous to their own well being, although I don't see just how he could harm them. We'll protect Germain, on the other hand, by telling them that he may be able completely to fathom the secrets of the ancient mech by means of his teleperception, and thus be able to repair them for the first time, or at least to guide *them* in the repair work. That would prove interesting to them, I am sure, as they are no longer immortals due to imperfections in their ancient mech. There is too much radioactivity, according to Svenga."

Nicholas thought a long time. Then he smiled grimly. "Yes," he said. "It might work, after all. It would certainly control Germain. Good. I'll contact Svenga immediately. He must by now have returned from his secret mission... I'll speak with New Moscow on the lunar beam."*

SEVERAL nights later, Stephen Germain fully regained consciousness. He felt very well. His head was now completely healed. He was no longer strapped down in the wheelchair to which they had transferred him some time earlier. So he got up gingerly in the darkness of his cell. He flexed his aching muscles. Something was wrong about this freedom they were giving him. Were they crazy?

I think I'll blast them all tonight and steal a plane—he thought to himself.

"This you will not be permitted to do," said an unknown voice.

Startled, Germain turned about and looked in vain through the darkness. He saw nothing. Instantly, his ponderous mind was probing space, seeing what was in the very air. And in the same instant he felt his flesh creep.

There in the room beside him, visible only to his mind, was a ghoul. It was only about four feet high. It was dressed

---

*Lunar beam. Powerful high-frequency beams that break the Heavyside layer and reflect off the moon back to Earth. An actual plan for televising programs to Europe by lunar reflection is being worked on at the present time.—Author.

like a mediaeval monk, in a brown, hooded habit. But its face was not that of any creature that had looked at the altar of God.

Pale flesh that looked as though it had been rotting under planks. Bulbous, watery eyes that looked ready to burst. A flabby nose splotched and swollen with purplish veins. A mouth utterly devoid of any human expression. The lower lip was so ponderous that it hung down, revealing lifeless gums and only two remaining upper incisors, like those of a vampire. His most outstanding feature was that he looked far too old to be alive, as though he were being preserved by means of stimulants alone.

At once, something instinctive in Germain rose up and made him hate this monstrosity more than anything he had ever hated before in his life. Without hesitation, and on the crest of a tidal wave of unaccountable rage, he summoned all the psychic forces within him. For one brief moment the ghoul, himself, was startled to see a dim halo of light appear about Germain's great, scarred head. Then the bolt of mental force struck. It was a force that could have killed a dozen men easily, had they been within its radius.

But the little ghoul only stood there and grinned back at him—although with the trace of surprised respect on his evil-wise face.

"You fire stupidly upon my teleprojected image," he leered. "I am not real, you see." His red-rimmed watery eyes glowered at him like a pair of festering carbuncles. "But *this,* you will find, is real."

Germain, plainly and simply, screamed with pain. A bomb exploded in each and every one of his bodily cells. It was a pain so great that it was impossible to sense it and live. So Germain fell to the floor and died—or so it seemed.

"You fool," came the ghoul's voice in the darkness. "You were not to kill him."

"But I did not give him enough to kill him," protested the other voice, in a somewhat guilty tone. "He's tricky. He can do things—I mean, things that perhaps even the mech cannot do."

"Meaning what?"

FAR away beneath a mountain, in the actual abode of the ghoul, a thing happened which had never occurred in the entire amazing history of the cavern people. The horrible little fiend stood within the field of a teleprojection machine, arguing with its operator, who sat beside him at a huge console of instruments. Suddenly, their minds were filled with a thought that was beamed to them by a thought ray sentinel somewhere nearby.

There is alien thought among us!

The first ghoul, in the teleprojector, thought back—Locate it. Our lives are in danger! This Germain is more dangerous than we were led to believe even by our telepathic analyzers.

"What do you mean?" queried the second ghoul, aloud, from his seat at the teleprojector controls.

"I mean that our intended victim has accomplished what we cannot—*true* projection. If we destroyed his body at this moment, *he* would still live to avenge his death. He does not need his body!"

"You mean—"

"I mean that you and I are about to—"

The terrifying thought that had formed in the ghoul's mind was borne out in that instant to be valid. For both of them died, much to the amazement of the thought beam sentinels.

Never before had they seen or heard of a mentality that could invade their world and kill when and where he pleased.

THAT night, Nicholas the First was visited by a ghoul in

teleprojected form, but this time visible to normal eyes. The Dictator only had time to sit up in bed and stare before the image spoke.

"You have betrayed us," accused the ghoul. "You did not warn us of Germain's true powers, hoping no doubt that he would be moved to direct his attentions to us. A fine stratagem, we admit, but not clever enough. For he cannot attack all of us, and before he goes too far we shall have him where we want him, where he will serve us and assist us even against Agarthi."

The ghoul's sickening eyes blazed anger. "As for you and your feeble empire, we shall destroy it…"

Then he disappeared. Nicholas had never seen a ghoul from Svenga's famous caverns, yet the experience failed to stagger his mind. Men like Nicholas do not allow misfortunes to do them harm. They merely cast them off onto somebody else.

To this purpose, Nicholas got up and began to dress. He was thinking of Dr. Borg. That old devil should have told him Germain was capable of fighting even the dero, the ghouls of the caves, the age-long dreaded foes of Agarthi. If he had withheld this much from him, perhaps he had withheld other information as well—the gathering data on the spaceship, for example. For all he knew, it might be complete, and Borg was probably biding his time to trick him out of it. Well, the time had come to show Borg who was the Dictator, once and for all.

As Nicholas left his room, he picked up his golden radium pistol… Couldn't kill Germain, he thought. I won't try it, or even think it. But if Borg has those spaceship plans ready—

A NEW type of being visited Germain. Germain had revived now. He was back in his chair, mind searching far and wide, thinking astonishing things that he could never have imagined.

The being who visited him was also one of the evil race of the ghouls, but he seemed to be of a slightly higher type. Younger looking, but fully as evil in his cunning—even sharper in his thoughts. One of the leaders of the cavern race, thought Germain. He was an average sized man dressed in mediaeval type clothing, but at his hip hung a very futuristic looking weapon of some sort. His hair was black and long, as was his beard. His flesh was pale like the ghoul's had been, but his eyes were bright black and clear and piercing. He showed all his teeth when he spoke.

"You have a certain power to annoy us," he said. "Even to destroy some of us. But we are as numerous as a great national of people, and even you cannot destroy a large enough percentage to make any difference in the long run. Now I am not accustomed to this but—I have come to make a bargain."

"You can destroy my flesh, but I shall pursue you forever," said Germain, with serene confidence. He was filled with uncontrollable hatred.

"But suppose we—ah—had your dear wife among our pleasant company?"

Germain tensed at that. He was unprepared for it.

Suddenly, within his room he saw projected before him a scene of living Hell such as had not been imagined by Man since the days of Dante. He saw, in miniature, a cavern. It was approximately one half mile long by a quarter of a mile in width. In its center was a lake of hot water, which was kept just at the boiling point by volcanic action. Gaseous yellow vapors rose from its surface along with the steam and were wafted by some means of ventilation along the ceiling and up a shaft.

The lake was just shallow enough for a man to stand up to his neck in it, but nowhere could he find it shallower, for the shores were comprised of cliffs that dropped straight into the water. On top of these cliffs roamed a number of ghouls. They wandered among a number of unhappy victims, naked men and women taken from the surface world, in the *flesh* and not in spirit. These men and women walked as though in a trance, straight toward the edge of the cliff. Unhesitatingly, they jumped into the lake. And there they struggled and screamed. Some there were who turned red—boiled alive. But they did not die. For above them, on bridges especially made for the purpose, ghouls sat at huge machines and performed fiendish miracles. They controlled their victims' minds and made them do anything they wanted them to do. And they filled the lake with energizing, stimulative life rays which would not allow the men and women to die, in order that their agonies might be prolonged.

Abruptly, the scene changed. Germain's horrified and hate-filled eyes saw the interior of a luxurious cavern banquet hall. Here a great Bacchanalian orgy was being carried on. Hundreds of men, mingling with the ghouls as though of one race and mentality, drank flagons of wine and reveled in unspeakable horror. A very beautiful dancing girl, evidently from the surface world, was made to dance suggestively on the long banquet table, naked. The men around her poked at her and tripped her. Some broke glasses in her path, and others made her dance on the broken fragments. She stopped, crying out and pointing to great, bleeding gashes in her feet. One great brute of a man then climbed on the table and, encouraged by the satanic crowd, cruelly embraced her before them all. Then, to Germain's uncontainable horror, he took a sword from one of his companions and proceeded to chase the poor girl along the table. When he caught her, he hacked her to pieces, furiously, passionately, while the onlookers rolled off their seats with laughter or fainted from the excitement of their own perverted passion.

Above this scene, Germain's blasphemed eyes saw another nude woman lying dead and horribly mutilated, in the arms of a statue of Satan. Then the scene vanished.

"What you have seen is no dream," said Germain's visitor. "What you looked upon is real. It is going on this very minute. These are our little pleasures in life. Whereas you of the surface, and those pusillanimous self-styled 'saints' of Agarthi, spend your lives in what you choose to call constructive pursuits, we happen to be geared to do the opposite. So it is with the nature of the Cosmos. There must always be construction and destruction. For every force exerted there must be an equal and opposite reacting force. The one phase must complement the other. Since existence is balanced between these two extremes it follows that the one extreme is no worse or no better than the other. So ours is the way of all that you abhor. And into this world of pleasures we shall be moved to invite your lovely wife, unless you care to do business with us. Teleportation is simple, you know. Any time we need some new victims we take them. Your poor officials in the Bureau of Missing Persons hide more unsolved cases than they care to have the public know about."

Germain did not speak, because words failed him, but he thought, and the visitor received the weight of that thought, through the telaug beam that accompanied the teleprojection beams, like an unendurable blast of thunder: *I love my wife, but my hate for you and your stinking kind is much greater. Much as the man in me suffers at the thought of deliberately sending my wife to Hell, I will do it before I'll give one inch to you. But your devils can bear in mind that all who harm her will die. Of that, at least, you can be sure.*

At that moment, Germain's whole mind and body was suddenly invaded by a consuming vibration. He tried to fight it, but he did not know how. He tried to escape from his own body, as he had done before, but he could not. It seemed to be shaking him literally into fragments, this gigantic vibration. A hum like that of a transformer filled him. It seemed as big as the world. His being seemed to explode apart, scattering like dust into endlessness...

Where he had sat, a blinding sphere of bluish flame consumed the very air. And when the flame vanished, so had the chair—*and* Germain.

"Got him," said the dero.

"All of him?" came another dero's voice.

"Yes. His mind did not escape. He is no more..."

"Then let us take his wife, since there is no danger. Her furlough is over with now. She is at the front again, in Cuba. There are many logical reasons why she should turn up missing—lost in combat and that sort of thing."

"Yes. I'd like to see her dance on the banquet table of the Yearly Feast."

MAJOR SERGEYEV PAVLOVICH had begun to suspect that something in the way of intrigue was brewing secretly between Dr. Borg and the Dictator, that is, something more than usual. In spite of the glad tidings of victory and the promise of more to come, the two seldom were seen or would seldom speak to anyone. Often the light was on in the late hours of the night in the Dictator's room or in the doctor's laboratory quarters where the latter lived. It was a rather persistent scuttlebutt, which had almost acquired the proportions of legend that Nicholas had engaged in some sort of secret treaty that was not turning out so well. But Pavlovich, who now took a full measure of pride from the fact that he worked in such proximity to the Dictator, reasoned that anything which could cause the burning of so much midnight oil was worthy of his own attention, as well.

For this reason he had done some spying for which he could have been shot, and had he been any other person than the officer in command he might have been caught. However, he succeeded at last in discovering and perusing, to his overwhelming amazement, the doctor's diary. What this monumental little volume left unsaid his mind was left in a fit condition to imagine.

Main facts gathered were:

1. Germain was to provide a door of escape—a ship of space.

2. The world was going to be too hot for anybody to stay in once the cave-people started an invasion, which they undoubtedly would, now that Nicholas' success threatened to place the surface world under one government.

3. The plans for the ship were just about complete. Gathered from between the lines was the fact that Borg distrusted Nicholas' allegiance to himself.

Pavlovich's reaction was a complex of anger, admiration, wonderment—and distrust, especially of Germain. Foremost of his reactions was anger in the face of the Dictator's apparent betrayal of the New World State, also that if a secret escape was being prepared he, Pavlovich, had not been included. Secondly, he had never been able to quench the flame of hatred that had been burning inside of him for Germain. Now his fear and distrust of the latter served to fan the flame into homicidal magnitude again. He saw rather plainly that when the time came for Germain's murder, Borg and Nicholas would be afraid to try it.

As he knew nothing of Borg's plan to call in the cave-people to control Germain he surmised that if he, himself, performed the service, Nicholas might include him within his inner circle of those whom he planned to take with him in his escape. But he also knew that the time would not be propitious for killing Germain until the degravtity plate plans were complete. So, surreptitiously, he scheduled visits to Borg's diary and watched for any indication that the work was complete.

And one day he read exactly what he was looking for:

Germain finished his work. The dero can have him now, if they can take him. But we must get out of here at once. I feel that my hypnosis over him is never quite complete. Even the sleep gas now leaves his brain wave patterns dangerously near the level of consciousness. When the hypnosis wears off, or when he pushes it off, the dero are supposed to start watching him, but by that time at least I, for one, will not be here.

It was on the basis of this little exposition of facts that Pavlovich fabricated a little plot, which was rather bold in that it involved a twofold risk to his own life. First, he would try to kill Germain by catching him when he was asleep. Secondly, he would kill Borg. Thirdly, he would take Borg's diary to Nicholas to prove that Borg was plotting to go away, himself, with the plans for the spaceship. On the basis of this twofold accomplishment he would appeal to Nicholas to take him into his plans, as a sort of bodyguard who would spare the Dictator all personal risks by taking them first, himself. He harbored no loyalty or love for Nicholas, but he loved power and security and distinction. For these things he was willing to pay any possible price.

So the night came when Pavlovich set out, with a radium pistol, to end the life of Stephen Germain. That it was the same night on which the teleprojected images of the cave ghouls were in the latter's room he could not have known. Or if he had known it might not have altered his plans, because one fault with Pavlovich, among others, was that he stayed fixed in a line of action until the end. Once he started out to get Germain there was nothing but his own death which could deter him.

It was due to this combination of circumstances that Pavlovich arrived at Germain's cell just after the bluish flame had wiped out all trace of him. Pavlovich sensed that

Germain was not on the alert, as he came near, because anyone who entered Germain's sphere of vigilance could feel his mind being probed by some indescribable psychic force. This night he experienced nothing, so he assumed that his intended victim was under another spell of Borg's hypnosis, and he decided to act swiftly while the opportunity lasted.

He opened up the door of the cell and made ready to fire at where he knew Germain would be sitting. He was going to fire without turning on the light, but he saw a small fire eating quietly away at a few shattered fragments of furniture. He also smelled materials burning, and he recognized the accompanying odor of ozone.

He dropped his gun hand and turned on the light to stare in amazement at the damage wrought. He was experienced enough in ordnance to realize that the damage created here had not been caused by death ray, machine pistol or grenade. Someone with a new type of electrical weapon had just wiped out Germain, and an admirably thorough job it was. But who? It could have been either Borg or Nicholas, if they had such a weapon. Or had it actually been the deros whom he had read about in Borg's dairy? That was closer to being the answer. They, too, might have considered Germain too dangerous to live. No wonder Nicholas and Borg wanted to *get!* Pavlovich felt the hair on the back of his neck rise up in fear. He had an instinctive urge to run from this place.

Suddenly, however, he heard a startling sound. It came from Borg's office, which was close around the next corner off the main corridor of the subterranean hospital.

"Don't shoot," he heard a strained voice say.

Then he heard the *whap* of a radium bullet's explosion and he immediately surmised that Borg was a dead man. In the next instant he heard the sound of drawers being opened and closed, plus the rustling of papers. So he stepped forward, intent upon making the most of an unexpected opportunity.

Especially would it be an opportunity if Nicholas were as yet unaware of Germain's death.

NICHOLAS looked up from the spaceship plans to see Pavlovich standing in the doorway of the room. The big fellow smilingly pointed a radium pistol at him. He had seen a blasted and disfigured corpse lying under one of the tables but he ignored it. His beady eyes were trained on those of the Dictator.

Nicholas' hand was on his gun, but it would have been risky for him to raise it at that moment.

"You are looking at your devoted servant," said Pavlovich, taking the initiative. "I have seen nothing." His eyes looked at the spaceship plans, then back at Nicholas, who had not yet moved a muscle or made a sound. Pavlovich had to struggle against the dominance of those terrible eyes, which seemed to possess the hypnotic powers of a serpent. "I—I have read Borg's diary, because I suspected him of treachery," he said. "I know what's going on and I don't blame you for wanting to pull out of here. But I want you to cut me in on this deal, Nicholas, I mean sir." Pavlovich swallowed hard. Those mad eyes were wearing him down. He never knew how much the Dictator could look like Satan, himself, with his pointed face, his sharp mustachios and spiked Van Dyke. "I came to kill Borg, myself."

"*And* steal these plans?" Nicholas accused, tonelessly. His hand gripped his pistol tightly, but he still did not lift it off the table.

"No," said Pavlovich. "I came also to kill Germain for you, and to give you the plans, because alone I could not have made much use of them. You or somebody like Borg, maybe, are the only ones who could have made real use of them—in short enough time."

This latter statement made sense to Nicholas, so he

concentrated on the previous one. "We've got to clear out of here," he said. "Germain may wake up any minute."

"You are afraid to kill Germain," said Pavlovich, "but while you let him live you are in double danger. If he dies you have only the dero to worry about. Let me contribute to your plans by killing Germain. After that, I'll take any other risk you want me to. I'll be your special agent and bodyguard. But I'm asking you to cut me in on this escape business."

"Go quickly then," said Nicholas, "and kill him." He, too, sensed that Germain's mental guard was down, otherwise he would have striven to subdue even the thought of aggression against him.

Pavlovich saluted. He turned quickly and disappeared. Tensely, Nicholas stepped to the door and listened. Soon he heard the door of Germain's cell swing open and simultaneously he heard Pavlovich fire. He heard him fire again and again, an unnecessary number of times, enough to blast his victim into untraceable fragments.

There was one tense moment, after that, of deep silence. Then Pavlovich said, "It's all over with, sir."

Nicholas thought: I could shoot this stupid ox, but he has the plodding mentality of a faithful dog. Maybe he will be useful, after all—for a while, anyway.

He stepped to the doorway of Germain's cell and looked in. The light was on, revealing a much-blasted room with no traces of the corpse left. Even much of the furniture had been blasted into small fragments.

"You shot him up well," he said. In his hand was the roll of plans that Germain had subconsciously prepared. "Come on, Major," he said. "You are in with me, as my special aide and bodyguard. Your lips are sealed on this matter, under penalty of death."

"Yes, sir," sang Pavlovich, elatedly, as he followed the Dictator out of the hospital. He dreamed already of New

Moscow, which he had not seen since its name had been altered. He palated, mentally, the distinction of being so close to the Dictator of the World, and he liked it. Life sang in his ears...

Nicholas stopped him for a moment. "Did you think that the corpse that you saw in there under the table was Borg's?"

"Why—yes, I—" The question startled Pavlovich out of his dreams.

The Dictator shook his head, manifesting a disappointed scowl on his hatchet sharp face. "Borg fled in haste, taking latest information in his head. That was an assistant of his that I shot. Borg is a very brilliant man, and he will work fast. We must do likewise to beat him at his own game, because I feel he is not up to any good—as far as we are concerned..."

CHAPTER NINE
The Prophecy Holds

IN AGARTHI, beneath the youngest mountains of the world, the most advanced scientists on Earth or beneath its surface were bustling with activity. In a certain cavern, which was filled with colossal machines that were almost as ancient as the young mountains, six of their number busied themselves earnestly over a myriad of delicate controls.

Behind them stood a tall, vigorous, youthful looking man who was yet old with centuries of wisdom. He stood patiently and watched them. It was the beginning of a new era for Agarthi. For the prophecy this man made years ago was coming true. The King of the World smiled to himself at the strangeness of truth that surpasses imagination. A common surface man had suddenly risen in an hour of need and appeared to possess powers that might even prove useful to Agarthi. The time had arrived for the fulfillment of the prophecy, for this new Prometheus was soon to join forces with those who represented Man's last hope.

One of the scientists who worked at a hugely powerful thought-beam machine (telaug), suddenly bent forward over the controls of another machine at his side and watched a teleprojection machine in front of him.

"I have the contacts," he announced to the others. "Watch."

The other scientists immediately left their own machines and came to the aid of their companion. One of their number silently took his place at other control panels beside the teleprojector.

In the screen there formed a vision of Germain in his cell at Santa Cruz. In front of Germain they could see the image of a dero talking to him. They saw also the images of the cavern Hell, which were being shown to him.

"They are going to dis-ray him," said one of the scientists.

"Quick, then," said the King of the World. "Use the teletransporter. It is his only chance." The King, remembering the prophecy, had confidence that the newly supercharged teletransportation mech's vibrations would be able to reach Germain.

The second scientist who had taken over controls next to the teleprojector now sprang into action. Behind the phalanx of tremendous machines a certain metallic cell began to glow with energy. Across the world went an invisible bridge of beamed vibration, vibrations minus quanta, hungry vibrations, seeking the quanta of energy that would complete them and make them true waves.

After some seeking, the end of this beam focused upon Bolivia, then upon Zone Seven, then upon Santa Cruz, and finally upon Germain.

"Concentration—up seven hundred," said the scientist.

One of his companions swung a dial and watched gages. "Seven hundred increase," responded the latter.

"Energize," cried the King of the World.

What followed occurred one split second before the dero fired their deathblow at Germain. The matter of Germain's physical being was vibrated so rapidly that its components gained mass. They gained so much mass in the tiniest fraction of a second that the equation of Relativity took effect, where matter turned to energy. Had Germain remained in the state of pure energy for more than the fraction of a second, he would probably have never lived again, for while he was in that state, he was dead, completely annihilated. But the god-like beings that had made the teleportation mech had discovered that life, mind, and soul are apparently subject to laws akin to inertia. They do not snap out instantaneously. No matter how violently a person may be destroyed or shattered, life, mind, spirit, all of them, hover for a moment, with the remains. It was that fraction of a second of life's inertia which had made the teletransporter possible, for before life, mind and spirit departed the teletransporter ceased its vibrating, thus allowing energy which had been matter (now in the state of quanta) to become matter again. While in the state of energy, the transporting waves could throw the quanta back to the generating, mechanism. Separate beams, working parallel with the teletransporter, always copied the image of the subject, in three-dimensional form, in a special force field, which was used as the receiver. The received quanta were then forced to return into the same relationship as before, and the end result was a transportation, through the ether, of the object, ending with perfect physical materiliazation. Life, mind and spirit took up where they had left off but a fraction of a second previously...

GERMAIN had no way of knowing that in less than a second he had been transported from Santa Cruz to somewhere inside the Himalayas. He shuddered from his recent experience and tried to gather his wits. When he looked around he found himself seated on the polished floor of a glass-enclosed chamber. Some very decent looking chaps in white robes were opening up the cage. Their robes were of clearest white, and all of the robes were emblazoned on the back with a great golden sword.

Behind them stood an amazing fellow who was at least a head taller than any of the others. He wore a golden yellow robe, which was held together by a belt that had green emeralds for tassels. He looked as though he could have answered any question a man ever had to ask.

This fellow looked at him with eyes that seemed to be able to see the marrow of his bones. Germain sent his mind out to him but was met with a great white mental wall. He could have blasted it, he knew, but he caught an unmistakable feeling of friendliness—a pure lack of deceit and vanity and selfishness that he had always found before in some measure in the minds of others.

You are among the sincerest friends you ever had, came the King of the World's thoughts, booming quite powerfully into his mind. *We have sent for you because we need you as much as you need us.*

Where am I? queried Germain, refraining politely from delving into this likeable fellow's mind.

This is Agarthi, replied the other. *You will be duly indoctrinated as soon as possible for there is no time to waste. Our common enemy grows stronger and bolder with each passing day.*

What is it you want me to do? asked Germain.

We do not know, replied the other. *It is in the prophecy that you will do some great deed to help us, to strengthen our arm against the dero. And we await this deed anxiously, for we know that the dero are quickly gathering forces to strike a deadly blow at the surface world. What it is you will do to help us must remain to be seen.*

Germain thought to himself for a moment. Then a smile suddenly lighted his face. *I have been playing around with a crazy idea,* he thought back at the King of the World. *Maybe you fellows are just the ones to help me out.*

The gathered scientists, who were also aware of Germain's telepathic message, looked at their leader in open admiration. "The last link of the prophecy," they said to him.

The King of the World only smiled and reached out his hand to help Germain to his feet...

MICHAEL KENT felt now that there were no further depths into which despair could sink. He had just received an official message in Miami that Lillian had been lost in action. She was not on the list of those killed. She was reported missing, and she had been missing for more than a week.

There could be little doubt that she had been killed, because half her outfit was wiped out in a recent Russo-Asiatic combined bombing raid on Havana.

Kent slumped down in his bed and wished he could sink through it into a bottomless pit. He foresaw America's defeat. His most cherished friends were cancelled out—gone from his life. There was nothing left for which to live.

He turned out his light and lay in darkness, enveloped in a dull stupor that was induced by bitterness and sorrow. He had never bawled since passing his twelfth birthday, but as he fought to swallow a stinging lump in his throat he wondered if that record was about to be broken.

Slim! Slim Kent! Take hold of yourself, old man!

Kent knew that intruding mentality. He opened his eyes wide in the dark, his heart suddenly leaping into double time. "*Steve,*" he gasped aloud. "My God! You're still alive…"

Very much so, thanks to a very fine group of friends I've run into, replied Germain. Kent was puzzled by the faintness of the telepathic reception. These thoughts seemed to be coming from a greater distance than that which lay between Bolivia and Florida.

No, replied Germain, reading his thoughts, *I am no longer in Santa Cruz. To tell you where I am, or where Lillian is, I—*

"Lillian!" exclaimed Kent. "You mean to say—"

We are wasting time, came Germain's thoughts. *Lillian is alive but in grave danger, but so is the world. I'm working to save them both and you may be able to help me.*

"Thank God she's alive Steve," said Kent. "But how could I possibly help you? You know I'm willing, and I'd give my life in a split second for you or Lil, but I feel so cockeyed puny and helpless."

You won't be after you've been indoctrinated.

"What's that?"

You can be of no help to us until you have been indoctrinated.

Prepare for a psychic experience, Slim. It will be quite a heavy one, but we've got to start at once. Close your eyes and relax. You are about to become a privileged visitor to the Seven Towers...

KENT had no time to reply. He dropped into a deep slumber and began to have a dream that seemed to be reality, itself.

He felt himself pulled, as though up a black and nebulous hill, out of darkness into dim, bluish light. He stood as though in another world or dimension. It was beyond his full comprehension. In all this world there was nothing except him, and a bluish sky devoid of sun, moon, or stars. He was a lone entity in an endless waste. He stood as though on blue clouds which stretched upward into unseeable distance, without horizon. Compelled to do so by an extraneous force, he walked forward, not knowing toward what.

Soon, however, there emerged out of nothingness, as though it were a mirage, a gigantic mountain of the blue mist. The mountain seemed man-made, for it was geometrically terraced, or pyramided, in six great steps. Before him, beside the first gigantic step, was a massive looking tower, windowless, uninviting. Its soaring top was on a level with the first step, and up on that first step he saw another tower, which began where the first had left off, and its top, in turn, reached the second step of the mountain. Above these two he counted five more, he thought. They faded upward into mists of distance...

CHAPTER TEN
The Seven Towers

AS HE looked at them he knew that his purpose in this strange place was to climb these towers, one by one. Although again he knew not why, he walked forward and approached the first massive structure that stood at the base of the mighty mountain.

The First Tower

HE stepped through its portals into vastness. The interior of the tower was like the interior of the mountain; nay—of the very world; or did he see Infinity, itself, stretch out before him? There was something that strangely distorted his vision as he walked into the tower and across its sagging floor. He seemed to grow smaller. The floor seemed to curve downward into a deep bowl of foggy night. It was an exceedingly unpleasant sensation, but he pushed onward, driven by an irresistible force.

Faster he walked, yet smaller he grew and farther the distance seemed. Also, shrouds of fog darkened his mind and he fought against it. He was so tiny now that the walls of the tower were lost to his sight. He walked as though through Eternity into the Sub-cosmos. After walking, it seemed, forever, he came to what he knew was his immediate destination.

There on the floor at the bottom of the bowl, not ten feet from him, was a strange little man who sat on a red and yellow carpet, smoking a water pipe. But he was only an inch high. As Kent approached him, with each step he, himself, grew smaller, until when he at last stood next to the man, he was no taller than he.

The man was old. His nose was red, his eyes a faded blue.

He wore the costume of a fool, a jester, complete with curled up shoe toes and bells.

"'Who are you?" he said to this man.

The other jingled his bells and said, "I am Man."

"So I am a man," retorted Kent, "but—"

"Oho! Oho!" laughed the jester, his bells clanging cheaply and dissonantly. "But you thought you were a god, a superior being whose science and wisdom encompassed all things knowable. There could be nothing new under the sun for you because you could always reduce the Unknown to conform to what you could understand. This method of self-blinding you called *science.*"

The fool sprang to his feet, did a clumsy somersault and made a clumsier curtsy. "But only *this* you really are. And only because you are so vain in what you consider to be your worldly knowledge. In order to see yourself face to face, as you truly are, you had to grow smaller, to a size that is unimaginably small. Man, for all his vanity, is a cheap, self-deceived, self-blinded fool."

Kent grew angry. Pride leaped within him and he lunged at this irritating Jack-in-the-box. But the "Jack" sprang out of the box and was suddenly nowhere to be seen. Kent then turned around to see a swampland stretching out behind him. He knew it was mental trickery, but he was forced to appreciate its reality to his mortal senses. There on the shore before him sat a huge, stupid-looking frog.

"Har-rump!" croaked the frog. "I am the wisest of all creatures in the universe. The universe, of course, is this swamp. I have lived here for three score years and ten. I know every pebble in it, every clump of rushes, every rotten log, every turtle and fly. There is, therefore, nothing more to know, and since I possess all knowledge I am the greatest of all living creatures. There is no greater perfection."

Just then a very incongruous thing occurred. Kent saw a

fleet of four-motored bombers, in miniature, sail right through the frog. They came out of nothingness and went into it. Immediately, he was moved to call the frog's bluff. He smiled proudly.

"What about four-motored bombers and all the modern technology of them, and their electronic controls? What do you know of that, oh frog who thinks he is so great?"

"Har-rump," said the frog, as unperturbed as a mountain. "Since I know all things already I cannot accept the possibility of the existence of things outside the sphere of that knowledge. What you mention is impossible. It cannot be. In fact, it angers me to hear such an idea even expressed. The thought is entirely revolting. You should be ostracized for not accepting present concepts as they are."

The frog and swamp then disappeared and Kent found himself surrounded by a myriad of jesters, jangling their bells and leering at him.

"Impossible! Impossible!" they chanted, in a mad, discordant song. "It cannot be! Why can't it be? Because it wasn't before! So therefore it is impossible. Impossible. *Impossible!* IMPOSSIBLE!" they roared, until Kent had to hold his ears.

There came a clap of thunder, a blinding flash of lightning, and Kent staggered back. Towering mightily above him was a giant jester who stared angrily down at him, legs spread apart, arms akimbo. When he spoke, his voice rang hollowly through the tower, as thought it were a voice of death inside a vast tomb.

"Man! Man! When will you ever know that while you sit like a self-satisfied frog in your slough of Ignorance there are things so much vaster than you passing around your head that they shrivel you into the insignificance of dust. Wake up! Open up those eyes which you, yourself, have willfully shut. Your only chance for gaining stature is an upward climb to greater knowledge. So climb, Man, climb!"

BEFORE Kent appeared a spiral staircase, and he ran to it readily, because he wanted nothing more than to be out of this place. He ran up the stairs, and as he climbed them they grew larger, as did he, until it seemed undignified for him to run. By the time he came to the exit on the roof tower, he walked with the calmness of a neophyte in godliness. He was leaving all of Man's blinding ignorance below in the Pit of Vanity. He had graciously opened his mind to Truth. And he knew somehow that the beginnings of great truths and revelations would be found in the second tower.

He came out through the tower's roof and looked over the parapet at the mist world below. He could see nothing. Somehow he felt elevated spiritually, and he took it as a sign of good that he could no longer see the mists that he had left behind. He crossed a perilously narrow bridge and passed between two massive pillars...

The Second Tower

THIS place was larger than the first. But instead of making him feel smaller it had the opposite effect. As he wandered across its floor he felt it rise convexly, and as he rose with it he seemed to grow still more. The illumination here was not so dim. It was bluish light, but brighter than before, and his vision was sharper, his step more sure. He walked on with increasing exhilaration and confidence.

At the top of the vast, convex mound that was the floor, he saw another man, a man who merely stood quietly waiting for his approach, as though he had nothing better in the world to do. But this man was no ridiculous, vanishing Jack-in-the-box with fool's bells round his neck. He was large, larger than Kent, yet as Kent stepped up close to him Kent grew sufficiently to match the other's stature. This was the same type of optical illusion as before, but in reverse.

The man was vigorous-looking, strong, healthy, cool and calm. He had the perfect, powerful symmetry of a god. His head was quite large, as were his age-wise eyes. For although he appeared to enjoy an undying youth, one could measure his centuries of life by the aura of wisdom which he wore.

His clothing was distinctly of the future. An emblazoned star of precious stones rested an the massive square of his chest, underneath a crystal-clear plastic blouse which was so pliable that it rippled like water with his slightest motion. He wore metallic woven trunks and a simple belt of gold. On his feet were sandals laced to the knees. His short-cropped hair was blond.

"Who are you?" said Kent.

"I am Man," replied the other. He raised his hand as Kent began to form a further question, for he read the thought in his mind. "I am Man after his awakening from Ignorance. Superstition, Fear and Vanity, I am Man advanced one hundred thousand years by the forces of Wisdom. Let me show you how I came to be. It all follows laws of natural development and, since you are no longer blinded by the Ignorance which is Vanity, and since your mind is open to the possibility of the truth, you will not deny that it can be so. Behold!"

Kent looked where the man's finger pointed, and he saw woven in the bluish air of the vast place the three-dimensional tapestry of things to come. Or so it seemed.

He saw the years of Man pass in massive, kaleidoscopic scenes of war and destruction, peace and social integration. However, this did not appear to be precisely the history of the nations of Earth as he knew them. It seemed to be a figurative history of Man, in a general sense, or as of Man evolved *somewhere else,* not necessarily an Earth.

HE SAW unimaginable progress toward godliness, while his strange guide, or host, explained: "Once Man evolves, wherever it may be in the universe, or the Sub-cosmos, or the Super-cosmos, he spends usually a quarter of a million years or so as a purely physical creature, depending on various factors which are in the majority influenced by the radiations of the particular sun under which he lives. For all his technical progress he remains a mere bundle of ganglia, nerve cells responding to stimuli, like a glorified vegetable. Each day of his wakeful life he devotes to the pursuit of the prime physical necessities: food, clothing and shelter. And his diet and habits of health and his ignorance in regard to medical science contribute to a low level of life expectancy, even in spite of beneficial sun radiations.

"Wisdom is the first step toward peace, security, physical emancipation and the next phase of Man's development. But Wisdom cannot be taught or learned. It is acquired through years of experience. It can be written down in books, but who can capture its true significance but another wise men? Therefore, while Man's individual life span is short the wise men are too few and too aged to ever assert themselves effectively. Ignorance continues to govern Man's actions and he passes inevitably through a period of self-destruction.

"Then one day he learns how to take better care of himself. He purifies his diet, subtracting insoluble fats and salts, and he advances in medical science. He stops using metallic substances and other non-organic materials as medicine and learns how to employ specialized human cells and natural processes in order to achieve health. If some of the sun's radiations are unhealthful, he shuts them out, likewise, allowing only the beneficial ones to reach him.

"As a result, he ceases to age. But as age is relative to size, growth must gradually continue with continuing youth. It is like mass and inertia. Small things have a small age. You have said that Man's years are three score and ten, yet the Earth's age can be measured in millions of years. It is proportionately larger. Growth cessation in Man is the announcement of his mortality. He will surely die if he stops growing. For when growth stops, youth is gone.

"Therefore, immortal Man must grow. He becomes gigantic, like a god, and he must seek new worlds in which to live. The stars of space exist in endless number. They are suns like your own—or better. About them revolve unnumbered worlds, many of them far better than Earth.

"With increased life comes the stabilization of Wisdom and its domination of Ignorance. Thus Man ceases to destroy himself. He puts the machine to work to produce his prime necessities and thus frees himself from physical work. He is ready to enter the mental phase of his evolution.

"He becomes a mentalist, magnifying his findings with thought-projecting machines, dream-making machines and mental conditioner machines. He can read his fellow's thoughts, so that all hypocrisy and deceit must vanish. So he progresses on the road toward godliness. He is great and powerful of stature, he is wise and endless in years, he can traverse the void of space to any star he pleases, he possesses the knowledge of life and death and can even create life out of inert matter. In short, Man can become a god. And this, in fact, is his goal."

By this time Kent was looking upon a marvelous machine world that created miracles that, to his own senses, were godly doings. He was looking upon the very life of the gods, beyond words to describe. His spirit was filled with a joyous hope for Man's future.

Suddenly, the pictures vanished, much to his regret. "You have seen the ramifications of truth-seeking—the partial extension of, the *possibility* of Man's progress. Now you must pass on to specific truths and learn something of fact which has already come to pass on your own world."

KENT felt himself rising in the air. He rose swiftly, supported by an invisible force. And as he rose, he also grew. Size was infinite, and time was eternal, he thought. A great exhilaration filled his being. In the first tower he had been cleansed of Ignorance and Vanity. In the second tower he had been treated to the wine of knowledge improved by Wisdom's aging.

He emerged on the roof of the second tower and unhesitatingly crossed the bridge to the third...

The Third Tower

THIS was the largest tower he had seen.

It was so vast that he could not see its farther wall. And he knew at once by the aspect of the place that here was proportionately far more to be learned.

He walked upon a vast desert in a greenish yellow light. Some giant hand had written on the sands before him: THE SANDS OF TIME. His footprints, as he progressed, left a lonely track behind him.

But this desert was by no means empty. He walked through the most gigantic wax museum that he had ever seen. Statues of men, women, horses, buildings, wagons, ships, and an endless variety of other things marched away on either side of his path to far horizons. No matter how far he walked, he found himself surrounded by this beautiful, paralyzed pageant. At even intervals he passed what seemed to be a sort of marker stone, giving the date. One he read said: THEREFORE 1800.

He stopped and looked back a few paces at some of the marvelous statues and structures he had passed. Not far back he saw unmistakable signs of the War of 1812, in the 19th century section. More than halfway back he had seen the Confederate soldiers of the Civil War. He knew that his eyes were being treated to a greater historical pageant than most men had ever dreamed of. He was literally walking down the halls of History.

In awed silence and with reverent step, he walked slowly onward. When he looked at the back of the marker stone he read the word: BECAUSE. He was going backward through history, for he recognized now certain outstanding characters and events of the 18th century (1700-1800).

He saw the French Revolution, even came upon the astute Voltaire hard at work by candlelight. And he came upon Washington and saw the Battle of Independence. He saw the faces of Suffering and Idealism and Hope. There was also James Watt at work on his steam engine.

He wanted to pause especially before statues of Catherine the Great, Frederick the Great, and Maria Theresa, which were all exquisitely perfect and complete with real jewelry, but some mysterious force drove him rapidly onward, and before he knew it he passed another marker: THEREFORE-1700. On its reverse side he saw again the word: BECAUSE.

Here he rushed through English history and out of the corner of his eye caught certain early scientists doing things. He walked through the middle of hellish scenes from the Thirty Years War, passed the sixteen hundred marker and recognized the pirates under Pizarro in their conquest of Peru.

Between each marker was such a world of events portrayed that he could have spent a year in each section without regret. Yet something pushed him onward, faster and faster, as though all this did not matter as much as what was yet to come.

And so he passed Gutenberg at his printing press, and Columbus on board his ship. He saw the fall of

Constantinople, the towering castles of feudal times, the Crusades. Faster and faster he went, through the decline of the Roman Empire into its heyday; even the life of Christ flitted by him without a moment to spare.

Now the marker stones went up in number: THEREFORE-200 B. C., 300 B. C., 400 B. C. He caught brief glimpses of Greek, Roman and Egyptian wars, passing almost by whole millenniums of time across the endless sands. He saw the pyramids and the sphinx in their building by a strange and beautiful *non-Egyptian* people, Moses and the Exodus from Egypt, even the Tower of Babel.

But now something new occurred. The marker stones appeared less taken care of and more broken down. The statues and scenes on either side of his path were not too well arranged any more. Some had fallen over into the dust. Some lay half-buried and unrecognizable. The BECAUSES and the THEREFORES were getting confused and hard to find.

He heard the hollow sounds of temple pillars crashing ponderously to the ground. The ground, itself, trembled, and he felt apprehensive. Were the sands of Time running out? Where did they lead from here? If he remembered correctly, he would soon come—

He heard it—*the roar of the waters.* It was the great flood of ancient times. He stopped, uncertain, unwilling to go forward. But he was pushed forward.

HE TOPPED a low hill to look out upon the angry waters of the Diluvium, itself. The surf below was washing the nondescript ruins of a mighty city. Everything in that city had been reduced to ghastly rubble.

On the shore amidst the ruins sat a man in robe and sandals who had a white beard and a balding head. He looked up at Kent and beckoned to him, as though he had been waiting for him for some time.

"Look at this chart," he said, as Kent approached. And he held up a large scroll on which it seemed he had been working. Kent looked at it and saw a long black line, which was labeled *800,000 years*. Toward the right end of the line he saw a small vertical line, followed by the words: *10,000 years, modern Man's written history*.

"Eight hundred thousand years!" exclaimed the old man. His sad eyes looked at Kent reproachfully. "For eight hundred thousand years Earth has been completely inhabitable by human beings such as ourselves. Your written history covers hardly more than one percent of that time, yet you pride yourself in knowing so very much about everything. How far does your knowledge reach beyond the Flood? If it reaches at all, the most important features are cast aside as parables."

"What are those important features?" queried Kent.

The man's eyes burned with enthusiasm. "That *giants* walked the Earth," he said. "They were god-men, those giants. Come, cross the flood with me and I shall show them to you,"

On the shore nearby was a boat with oars. Kent knew he was to cross the waters in this skiff, so he stepped toward it without hesitation. The old man followed, like the boatman of the River Styx. And he thought how true it was that Man knew so little, after all, concerning ancient times. A lot could have happened and been deeply buried in the Sands of Time, even hundreds of thousands of years before the Sphinx was ever thought of. For time was infinite with the Cosmos, and all was relative. In the past all things could have happened which will yet occur in the future…

When the skiff had worked its way well out upon the waters to a point where no land was in sight, Kent remarked about it to the boatman.

"No land?" said he. "Land ho! Land ho!"

And in that instant Kent saw land in two directions. He saw land rising up from beneath the ocean waves. Great tides were thrown back as two continental landmasses arose from the depths, one ahead and one behind.

"Behind us lies Atlantis," said the boatman, tugging resolutely at his oars. "Ahead lies Lemuria. These were ancient landmasses whose sinking raised the North American continent out of the water. Hence the legend of the Flood in all countries and among all races of people, for these continents were largely the home of terrestrial Man."

When they got to the shore of Lemuria they found it already clad in the dense verdure which belonged to a long gone prehistoric era. In those vast, post-carboniferous jungles roamed terrible and monstrous beasts. This period surely belonged to one beyond the ken of human knowledge, immeasurably lost in the past, thought Kent.

"You are no longer going backward in history," explained the boatman, walking with him up the shore. "Here you see it rapidly, but in chronological order. Behold," he said, pointing to the sky.

KENT looked up and saw, to his astonishment, an uncountable number of very beautiful vessels, which looked like mighty submarines. At first, they were only tiny specks in the sky. Then soon some appeared to be like toy models. Very quickly, however, he saw them sweep majestically overhead in gigantic, mile long proportion.

"At this time," explained Kent's guide, "Earth's indigenous humans were cave people dwelling in animal darkness. These advanced specimens of Man came among them like gods. They had had eons of time to develop in another part of the universe, until they became immortal wise men. But their own sun had grown old and begun to throw out too many rays which were detrimental to life, so they were forced to search for a new world in another solar system, far from their ancient home. This was the secret of their immortality, basically. For they knew that Creation surged on tides of disintegration and integration, destruction of matter and construction of matter. Whenever in one part of the universe the disintegration, with its harmful radiations, was occurring, in still another part an equal and opposite integration, with its accompanying beneficial radiations, was occurring. So they learned to follow the beneficial tides and never subject themselves to the disintegrant forces of nature. They traversed the terrible voids of the interstellar abyss, at speeds surpassing that of light, itself, and here they have found, at least momentarily, a new home.

"In those ancient days on Earth, the sun's rays were highly beneficial, and plant life was as irrepressible as animal life. Plant and animal alike grew to great sizes and lived to a great age. It was a fit home for these god-men of old. Because of their immigration to Earth your modern Earthmen still cherish legends of ancient gods such as Zeus, Thor and Wotan, with their might and their thunderbolts. Such supermen existed, as you see before you. Behold their progress."

Kent saw, with an accelerated historical perspective, how these giant, beautiful beings of another time rapidly created out of Earth's riotous jungles a heavenly Paradise. Great, glistening cities were built, in ages beyond reckoning before the Flood. These people prepared their diet, until they were pure and positively beneficial, extracting all sources of poisoning or insoluble residue. Such detrimental radiations as reached them from outer space they could shield out of their great cities by means of electrical force fields.

They lived and loved generously, wisely, without deceit or waste or evasion. They grew as eternally as they lived, and their god-like machines, which were but complicated extensions of their marvelous intellects, developed in size as necessity demanded. The machines were as eternal as their makers.

"However," said Kent's guide, "there came a time when three harmful factors had to be anticipated, and this brought about a great change. One factor was the sun. It was beginning to become detrimental like that previous sun they had left in ages past. Some felt that they would have to leave this otherwise beautiful world and seek again a home in space on another far-flung world. But others there were who did not wish to enter on the long star-road again. Instead, they proposed building a great empire underneath the ground, away from the sun's powerful detrimental rays, which now required too much force field energy to shield out. Below the Earth's surface, they could filter in only the good rays and supply a number of their own through artificial means. Their great disintegrator beams, which could melt mountains, could easily carve out vast caverns for them, and their integrator beams could then solidify the walls of those caverns until they were harder than steel and hundreds of feet thick. Even earthquakes and ocean's weight were no match for such walls.

"A second factor which influenced them to begin the construction of such caverns was the advent in Earthly skies of enemy races of supermen. Great wars ensued, and from these events you have derived the legend of the Battle of the Titans."

Kent gazed in awe at the spectacle of these actual wars. He saw these great men hurl bolts of death from their cities and ships, half across the world, shattering mountains and blasting cities out of existence.

"So the first god-like settlers of Earth prepared themselves an underground home. Their caverns eventually extended to most of Earth's then existent continents.

"But there came a third factor—geological changes. Lemuria and Atlantis were to sink and the American continent was to rise from the depths of the ocean. This and the factor of continuing growth finally led them to travel out upon the star-road after all."

KENT, to his sorrow, saw them depart in their thousands of great ships, leaving Earth to its upheavals and its poisoning sun which now brought early death to ordinary men and unprotected plants and animals. No more would the god-life flourish here. Only stunted and short-lived, life henceforth would be a farce, pointless because it was so temporary.

"From this point begins another phase of knowledge which you must absorb," explained the guide. "So go now to the fourth tower."

A great wind came and caught Kent in a cyclone vortex. Flood swept over the land of Lemuria beneath him and he shot upward. As though in a dream, he emerged and saw before him the fourth...

The Fourth Tower

THIS tower was darker and more forbidding in aspect, which caused Kent to hesitate, but again something drove him forward. He passed between great monolithic stones as though into a cavern. Several great bats flew out above his head. He felt as though he were underneath the ground. Great rocks, like small mountains, lay sideways on the ground, and he walked among them in the semi-darkness like a Lilliputian. This appeared to him to be a lonely place to which men should not come, akin to that land of shadows depicted in Grecian legend as the place of departed souls.

Soon there appeared before him, coming toward him on the shadowed path between the giant rocks, a man in a black robe. As the man drew nearer, Kent saw that he was sightless. His vacantly staring eyes were almost pure white, like scar tissue.

"Before you travel onward," said this man, in a sepulchral tone, "you must learn what I shall tell you now."

He motioned for Kent to sit down on a boulder nearby, just as though he could see without eyes. Kent sat down.

"Neophytes who enter the fourth tower," said the blind man, "have been purged of Vanity and are thus seekers of the Truth. They also have faith in the god-destiny of Man. And they have been given knowledge of the great Elder Race, of the ancient god-like beings who once lived on Earth and made of it a Paradise, beings who, wherever they may be living their heavenly lives today, are referred to by us as the Elder Gods. We do not worship these beings, but they serve as a pattern for that ideal Perfection which Man does personify as the One God. It is toward this state that Man must ever gravitate, because it is fundamental law.

"You have been shown how the Elder Race left the Earth. But now you must be told that there were certain less perfect members of the race who stayed behind, probably because they had quarreled openly with their superiors and were thus condemned to remain. These were, in fact, the 'fallen angels' of legendary fame. And they did go into the Pit, which consisted of the caverns beneath the Earth that the Elder Race had left behind. For here were all the great machines that were still in a fit condition to support them practically as they had the god-like race which had made them.

"But a great degeneracy crept upon them and, as your own Bible says, they 'looked upon the daughters of men.' That is, they married into the ordinary race of the indigenous Earthmen and thereby degenerated further.

"It was not long after this that the great geological change occurred. Earth's axis slipped from the perpendicular, and the jolt sank Atlantis and Lemuria. Millions of men and animals were destroyed.

"But some things survived to live in a very much poisoned world, where now, due to Earth's tipped axis, there was no eternal spring of Paradise, and the menacing rainbow rode the skies. The first appearance of the rainbow signified that the sun's carbon coat was gone and now that poisoning orb burned metals, casting out the deceivingly beautiful spectrum of *death*. Then truly were Man's years only three score and ten. He had degenerated to a stunted dwarf who died before he could find time to learn to think.

"But some there were who entered the ancient caverns of the Elder Race, through secret portals, and this is a fact which brought about the next most important phase of Man's history.

"At first, it was a relatively simple matter for them to run the great machines. The machines used water as fuel, breaking water into hydrogen and oxygen and thence operating atomically, using hydrogen as the end fuel. The fuel was always as limitless as the energy that these machines could release. They bathed the cavern people in beneficial stimulant rays and gave them a sort of synthetic immortality.

"But the ancient legend of Hell and the belief in the forces of Evil living in the Pit beneath the Earth owe their origin to the failure of these very ancient machines. Perfect as they were, if not properly maintained they would deteriorate through the ages. The deterioration came in the form of accumulated radioactive deposits in certain of them, especially those that performed telepathic or mental functions. The constant exposure to this type of poisoning created the *deros,* or devils.

"A dero is a *detrimental robot*. His thought may start out constructively, but due to a negative twist to his thinking caused by detrimental energy radiation from the machines, the end result is a destructive thought.

"So, whereas the surface man usually spends his time in constructive pursuits, at least individually, the cave dero spends his time just as busily and energetically in destructive or detrimental pursuits.

"Now, to become a dero was not always the fate of the cavern people. There were some who had machines which, due to various special circumstances, were not as heavily laden with radioactive deposits. These people early identified the true deros as enemies and succeeded in sealing themselves off in various places to live their own lives. These are called the *tero,* or beneficial robots, people who are still capable of dedicating their energies to constructive purposes. The surface man owes the tero much, but unfortunately the tero were fewer in number by far than the dero, and since those ancient times when the first mech or machine began to break down and emit detrimental energy, the dero has governed the affairs of men."

The blind man pointed like a grim spectre at a great, mountainous rock nearby, which towered upward into formidable darkness. "This way you must go," he said, "to learn how the dero has influenced man from the dawn of your own written history… Go."

KENT rose silently to his feet and turned resolutely toward the great rock. There he saw a stairway cut in the stone. It seemed to be incredibly ancient. He felt, as he started to climb it, like Moses ascending Sinai. He ascended into darkness and did not sense the old exhilaration. Rather he felt that the strengths given to him in the other towers would be needed to face that which was to come.

He emerged from the fourth tower and looked amazed at the fifth. It loomed above him like that secret entrance to Hell that Dante claims to have discovered. Nothing could have been as uninviting as that cavernous maw which seemed to yearn for his very soul. Yet he stepped across the tattered bridge which led to it and entered...

The Fifth Tower

WHEN he entered, he knew at once that he was in a place that was a facsimile of the Pit, or of the dero caverns beneath the surface of the Earth. Darkness more profound than that which he had encountered in the previous tower now confronted him. An uneven pathway led crookedly among fallen monolithic stones, and a ponderous ceiling arched low over his head like gathering clouds of doom. He sensed the terrible weight of miles of earth upon these rocks. Here, out of some deeper darkness before him, emerged the breath of Evil. His spirit cringed within him, out of revulsion more than fear, but still he was made by an unseen force to tread onward.

As he advanced into a more cavernous darkness his footsteps rang unaccountably, echoing back at him like the cacophony of demon laughter.

Suddenly, a black, gigantic shadow loomed up out of nothingness and the foul stench of a sweating beast filled his nostrils. The gigantic face that looked upon him was that of Satan. No man could look upon that evil countenance and retain his soul. Or so it seemed to him. He cried out in mortal terror while the vast shadow-demon before him shook the cavern with triumphant laughter. Satan pointed a finger at him, while his fiery eyes glared greedily, and Kent felt a coldness envelop him, accompanied by an imploding blackness.

Then, suddenly, he felt as though some hand had saved him, and he steadied himself. The vision of Satan vanished. In his mind he sensed a calm voice saying: "Even we do not tread the path on which you walk. But we shall guide and protect you as you advance to look upon that which surface men refer to as Hell. And you shall see that no terrifying imaginings of Man can do justice to this place. Advance!"

Kent walked onward, but only because he was forced to. In spite of the protection that had been offered him, he knew that he was in some real danger.

"The image of Satan," continued the voice of his protector, "was created out of the imagination of a clever dero. He transmitted this thought into a telaug or telepathic projector and, augmenting the image thousands of times by means of the machine, he directed it at your mind. Such rays can be directed upward toward the surface world and can cause many a man to go insane, shrieking that he is tormented by voices and monstrous images. Your insane asylums contain many such dero victims, who still continue to be tormented.

"From ancient times, when the Egyptians were first settling in the Nile valley, such rays of torment have been directed at surface men. Sometimes such dreams and visions have been made to materialize by means of the telesolidograph machine, which forms three-dimensional, opaque images. Thus began 'spiritualism,' which has been rightly termed by clergymen as *demonism*. For demons, or dero, are the masters of spiritualism by means of which surface man may be misguided.

"Through this means the next step was achieved. If the surface subject was willing to make certain concessions he would be given certain 'powers.' Through means of the teleportation apparatus, surface beings could be—*and still can be*—transported to Hell. Some famous witches have permitted themselves to be used in Hell in return for the 'Devil's' favors on the surface world. We shall show you an actual case…"

Suddenly Kent stood in a small cavern where he could look out upon a vast banquet hall and not be seen himself. A nondescript conglomeration of human beings dressed in mediaeval clothing and even ancient Roman costumes reveled about the feast table, drinking and carousing in the fullest tradition of ancient imperial splendor.

BUT there were some features of this banquet that had never been witnessed upon the surface of Earth. For, among other horrors, Kent saw a roasted girl served on a giant silver platter to cannibals. He wanted to retch, to turn away, but he was forced to see more.

All about these revelers at the table were dancing girls, most of them nude, who danced voluptuously to music which was designed to excite the erotic senses. There were also invisible vibrations in that room which excited these senses to an unimaginable extent. When men at the table grew tired of illicit food and drink (white wine reddened by human blood) they would avail themselves of a dancing girl, quite oblivious to the rest of the crowd.

These girls, wearing expression of delight, suffered the tortures of Hell, because they had to give themselves lest they be subjected to the greater tortures. There was one among them, however, whose soul was not tortured. She wore nothing but one diaphanous black veil, which swirled like a dark nebula about her too voluptuous form as she danced. Hers was a genuine pleasure when she yielded her special charms to the more privileged of the feasters. But this whore of Hell was so deliberately lewd that Kent refused to look. He fought the controls which had been placed upon him and closed his eyes.

"We are sorry," came the voice of his protector, "but we have spared you, really, from worse scenes. Look now and you will see something else."

Kent looked, hesitantly, and was surprised to be looking at the same lewd woman who had cavorted with men at the banquet, now dressed like a respectable Puritan woman, walking down a village street sometime back in the seventeenth century.

"Remember Salem?" came the voice, suggestively. And thus he knew that he was looking upon a witch, and he realized that his own sympathy for those Salem women, while reading history, because of their handling by "superstitious" and "ignorant" townspeople, had in some cases been wasted.

The woman walked with an air of chasteness, and passing villagers greeted her with respect, for she was the wife of one of the leading citizens. But when no one was near her expression turned to one of evil triumph. This night she would get rid of an enemy who knew too much.

When she got home, she took out of an old trunk a remarkable doll. It looked very much like the village preacher who had passed her on the way home. This she put some finishing touches to, and when night came she made some signs over it. Then she thrust a needle directly through its heart.

Kent then saw a dero in one of the caves. He saw the demon looking into a viewing screen, saw the image of the Puritan woman thrusting the pin into the doll.

"Katy communicates well," said the dero to some unseen companion. "She desires the preacher to die of 'heart trouble.' I wish they could think up something new. But 'tis always 'heart trouble.' Ah, well, as long as the stupid fools cannot devine the actual causes it matters not. Katy is great sport at the feasts. 'Tis always a great find to get a willing dancer rather than have to make robots out of the girls. As long as Katy remains young and beautiful and willing why should we not join her in her fun on the surface? Sure, let's kill the old— People always expect preachers to die prematurely, being so close to Heaven. They think it is respectable. Give him a jolt, will you?"

Kent then saw a bedroom where the preacher slept. The man's eyes opened, an expression of pain suffusing his countenance. Then he suddenly stiffened in death.

"So it was," said the voice of Kent's protector, "that the deros gave out nefarious assistance to those who would cooperate with them and keep a silent tongue in their heads. This intercourse between surface people and cavern people has been known variously as witchcraft, demonism, spiritualism, voodooism, clairvoyance, legerdemain, and black magic. But the dero of the caves made even a mockery of religion, inspiring directly the cruelties of the Spanish Inquisition, and the ancient Christian persecutions under the Romans.

"In every walk of life they have turned man from the paths of construction. Through the perpetuation of dogma and superstition they have deterred man in his due progress.

"Why is this? Because, in the first place, the dero wants nothing to do with our unfiltered sunlight. It would kill him quickly. He looks upon his cavern world as his salvation. But, in the second place, he is suspicious of surface man's progress. He fears that if he progresses far enough he may discover the dero and find some way to drive him out of the caverns. For this reason the dero take a direct hand in deterring man. Just what kind of a struggle is going on in modern times you must also learn quickly? It's because the struggle is rapidly approaching a dreaded climax. Come."

KENT found a path in the dark cavern, which led precipitously upward, and he climbed it gladly...

WHEN Kent climbed out on the roof of the fifth tower and looked at the sixth, he thought, for a moment, that he was looking at the Empire State Building, so neat and modern did it look. This place he entered much more confidently.

Once inside, he saw a welcome blue sky filled with aerial commerce. And before him stretched Chicago of 1970, as familiar to him as ham and eggs. He stood there for a long time contemplating the roaring rush of modern life that was Chicago. He thought of man's great forward strides in science and he wondered how the dero could fight modern man, and of how it would be to stuff a couple of atomic bombs down their throats.

Then he was suddenly confronted with a vision of deros in a cavern that he somehow knew was underneath Chicago. There were about a dozen deros seated around an ancient stone table, all of whom were engaged in earnest conversation.

"Modern man knows very much about science," said one of them. "He has already discovered atomic integration and disintegration. He has produced in his laboratories the phenomena of transference, whereby matter becomes energy."

"The outstanding feature is that he is a smart devil, surface man," commented another dero. "We fools down here can only rely on our one great asset—the ancient mech. With the mech we could still wipe out the surface world's civilizations. But we have actually slipped behind the surface man's progress in technical knowledge and skill, I believe there are some among them who might be able to reproduce, at least crudely, one of the ancient machines if they were allowed to examine it."

"Well, we have succeeded so far in tripping him up by

means of the pleasure technique," remarked another. "The production of juke boxes and motion pictures of the erotic and senseless type, as well as idiotic radio programs and insane jingle-jangle in their songs, has all reached a new peak, either in spite of or because of the war. The fools even bring jukeboxes and the silliest type of films into their army camps so that they can take the men's minds off the war. What imbeciles. If they only realized that it is *thinking* that we fear the most. But they cooperate beautifully. They all flock to anything that can nullify thought, to any means of killing time so that original thinking will not occur. It seems to me to be a very good safeguard for us, this consistent stupidity of man."

"But Nicholas the First will soon conquer even America," said another dero, "and under his rule men may actually have time to think, because he prides himself on his intellectuality and would ban anything but serious and educational pictures, even though they may be prepared by the State and hence quite biased. Juke boxes he would junk, and that has been one of our most successful instruments for sustaining zoot-suitism and jitterbugging.

"Nicholas' man Svenga has made a stupid treaty, offering us all the slaves and food we want. Ha! As if we couldn't take them anyway. Last week we raked in over a hundred Chicago beauties which the Bureau of Missing Persons obligingly turned into 'cases under investigation.' But they always give up, and they never get wise. If they do get wise, all we have to do is talk to them and give them a few wild dreams, and the 'law' again obliges us by putting such people into insane asylums. The more they know and try to tell, the more solitary becomes their confinement. Our absolute guarantee of safety is that ineradicable fatal vanity of his which leads him to believe that anything which he, himself, can't think up or invent is entirely impossible, and that if anybody believes otherwise he belongs in the insane asylum. I tell you, it's wonderful!"

"But we must strike at Nicholas' empire," said the first dero who had spoken. "Now is the time, while Agarthi still lies unprepared."

SUDDENLY the vision vanished from Kent's view, to be replaced again by the previous vista of bustling Chicago.

"And so it is," said the invisible guide to Kent. "Surface men today would place a man in the insane asylum if he spoke openly of these things. That is why not much progress has been made toward protecting man from the evil influences of the dero. As you heard one of them say, their greatest protection is man's own incredulity. It is that vanity which perpetuates ignorance. If what I am saying were written down for common men to read they would laugh at it in the ignorance which is vanity, *not knowing that it is a ghastly truth,* and that the dero rub their hands approvingly at such unbelieving laughter. Surface man obliges the dero, enabling the latter to even influence government, always leading man into the pathways of destruction and defeat.

"A grave danger thus threatens the world. With dis-ray the dero can cause whole cities like Chicago to vanish from the surface of the Earth. The reason they have not done this sooner is that the surface world supplies them with food for their sustenance and slaves for their pleasure. But more than this, Agarthi stands as a threat against them. For it can destroy many of the dero caves, being equipped with the best of the machines of the elder race. Unfortunately, those machines are too few and far removed from some of the scenes of action.

"But now you must know fully of Agarthi before you will be completely ready to be of service to us. Come..."

Kent saw a bright path of pure light winding upward into

the sky, and he followed it, as though he expected to see the pearly gates of Heaven…

The Seventh Tower

WHEN Kent stepped out on the roof of the sixth tower and looked at the seventh, he knew that he was about to enter Agarthi, itself. For there before him was an ancient entrance as though in the side of a mountain. And this entrance was shaped like the portal of a great temple, but in simple lines, in a style which was vaguely Mayan, minus the carvings.

As he entered he sensed at once a reassuring peacefulness and calm. Here was the quiet sanctuary of wisdom.

He walked down a great hall that was like a broad avenue. Beautiful, ancient cars rolled past him silently. Kindly looking people smiled knowingly at him from these cars as they passed. The place was filled with such a clean atmosphere and the streets were so immaculate that he felt as though he should remove his shoes.

But the same guiding force moved him onward. He walked into a great, softly lighted cavern and beheld a stone city of eternal beauty. Here was the beauty of simplicity. There was no crowding. Houses were spacious, filled with gardens and pools and fountains, lined with verandas and roomy roof gardens. Avenues were broad and the sidewalks roomy enough for streams of street traffic.

The whole city was built on a plan so as to converge toward a huge building at the further extremity of the cave. This was a tremendous palace, but more massive than it was ornate. Toward this, Kent's feet were forced to lead him.

In awe he climbed the seemingly interminable steps of this palace and entered a mighty doorway. Here were no guards standing about in traditional fashion, blocking his passage with spears or bayonets. For no weapons or guards seemed to be necessary. Only a kindly looking people passed in and out of the building, and all smiled knowingly at him as had the others in the cars he had seen in the streets.

Soon he found himself entering a great throne room, which was silent and empty. Empty except for one person, who sat on a great throne on a raised dais. This person was Kent's idea of the ultimate man. He looked something like the fellow whom he had met in the second tower.

"Who are you?" he asked just as he had asked the other.

"I am known as the King of the World," he said, in a calm, resonant and friendly voice. "I have had you brought here so that I might tell you something about Agarthi. Please be seated."

Kent, not finding a chair, sat down on the steps below the throne. The King of the World smiled at him in a friendly fashion and began his story.

"Long ago," he said, "when the Elder Race left the Earth to seek their home among the stars, there were some left behind who were not as degenerate as they had been judged to be. One or two of these great beings soon anticipated the very development of the dero, which you have witnessed. They were not able to stop the development, but they were able to educate their sons, born of Earthly mothers, to run the machines and take care of them. As time passed, these advanced tero found this cavern in the Himalayan Mountains, and they have remained here ever since.

"At first they planned only to seclude themselves from the dero and from man, as well. But as the ages passed they saw the terrible work of the dero progress, until they had to take pity on surface man for his plight, even in spite of the latter's persistent vanity and stupidity. So in recent times Agarthi has begun to prepare itself. The chief danger is that the dero still possess ancient ships of space. The dero are afraid of them because the elder race left them behind as 'defective.' Yet it is known that these ships are at least operative within the immediate effective range of Earth's gravitation, and with such ships the dero could concentrate their weapons above Agarthi and cause us great damage, even in spite of defense weapons. Or the dero could even escape to Mars or Venus, to return at a later date and torment terrestrial man. The only thing that those ancient ships cannot do is to achieve the sustained high velocities necessary to traverse interstellar space to other solar systems. If they could do that they should have left this solar system long ago.

"Now Agarthi has begun to build a fleet of new ships which would enable us to deploy our forces or, if things become too difficult, escape, ourselves, even to another solar system, if we dared undertake such a dangerous journey.

"But we of Agarthi would not abandon mankind. We believe that this Earth is still worth living and fighting for. True, the sun is poisonous, but with proper precautions a man could still live here for from three hundred to five hundred years. A Utopia could still be made here if we could rid ourselves of the deros. Then I, myself, would take over the world and make it that benevolent Utopia which I know I can make it.

"However, the actions of Nicholas the First, who is my rival in a way..." He smiled indulgently, "...have caused the dero to advance their plans at a time when we are as yet unprepared. If they were to attack us now—and they must surely attack us before they attack Nicholas because we will fight them, regardless—they would no doubt be able to destroy us. Then would man's civilization be truly ruined by them, at will, and with no further protection from Agarthi. The dero would thrive mightily in their caves, sucking like leeches at a defenseless mass of disorganized and helpless survivors."

Kent was moved to speak. "But what can I do to help in

all this?"

"Your friend Stephen Germain," replied the other, "has requested that you be indoctrinated, as he feels that it will make you useful to him and to us as a sort of personal 'in the flesh' representative in the United States. If there be any other reasons; they will be explained to you directly by Stephen Germain."

EVERYTHING suddenly faded into nothingness, and Kent woke up in bed to find himself wet with perspiration. His head ached dully. His mouth was dry. His legs felt numb.

"Steve!" he called, testily. "Steve…!"

That is all for now, came Germain's tired thought. *I need as much rest as you, so let's get some sleep. I will contact you further tomorrow. But I can tell you this much. I need you to make first hand physical contacts for me among government officials, as I find that mental contact only confuses them and makes them go see psychiatrists or suspect that they are insane; or if they did believe me others might think the wrong thing. So a strongly sympathetic physical front in the United States is what I need, and that's you. If I succeed in the thing I am going to attempt, I'll need some fast action on your part. Stand by, Slim…*

"But Steve, what about Lillian?"

I am protecting her as best I can. She is momentarily safe although in very undesirable surroundings.

"Steve. What is it you are going to try to do?"

I can't tell you now. However, I may not come through this thing. If I don't, then I guess our number is up—for everybody on the surface. Some Argarthians may escape into space. However, if I succeed, then I'll be seeing you…

"Steve!"

But Germain's thought was gone from Kent—just where, he could not know… Indeed, even Agarthi would not have been so bold as to divine correctly just where it was that Germain planned to go, much less the deros. Only one man knew, and that was Stephen Germain...

CHAPTER ELEVEN
King of Ghouls

LIEUTENANT Lillian Germain had reached the saturation point of battle strain. For twelve days and nights she had looked almost as much upon the entrails as upon the outward features of the fighting men and women with whom she lived and suffered. During that period, Cuban skies above her tired, disheveled and bandaged head had been filled with enemy bombers and strafers. There seemed to be no end to them ever since they took Caracas. She felt, as Kent had, that the end was inevitable, and that it was very near.

One night just outside Havana, near an anti-aircraft battery, she was caught in a particularly thick bombardment. Before, in other raids, she had recognized a certain factor of safety in the occurrence of the interstices between explosions. But this night the bombs seemed to rain down in an interlocking pattern. She sensed stronger than ever before the vivid reality of mortal danger in the growing thickness of the explosion pattern. She was suddenly paralyzed with the presentiment that this night her number was up.

She lay flat on her stomach, her wide, horrified eyes staring over dead bodies into a night of fire and annihilation. She saw three ambulances blast apart into dismembered automobile and human parts, gruesome pieces silhouetted too brilliantly against the flashing tapestry of destruction. The unsupportable, sound of it all welled up like a flood of molten metal in her brain. Destruction, like the phantom of Mars, crept nearer, closing her in a circle of disintegration. The sky shook with the sound of engines. The stars were gone behind a screen of smoke and fire—and a myriad of black wings. Ground rocket batteries flashed bravely back, then scattered like twigs in the wind before the demolition blasts.   Trucks and motorcycles gyrated crazily through craters where roads had been. Men ran between them. Then blue-white angry blasts wiped everything out before her, or wherever she looked.

She heard a soldier crying for home, his face groveling in mud. "Mom! Mom!" he sobbed, as though his heart had lips that spoke.

She tried to crawl toward him over the trembling ground and the half-buried dead.   Suddenly she herself began to shake. Her whole mind and body seemed to be consumed by an all-pervading vibration.   It seemed to shake her into fragments. The roar of a giant transformer drowned out the chaotic noise of battle. She held her temples and screamed as she sensed that she was literally flying apart...

MUCH to her surprise, she regained consciousness. Before she opened her eyes she experienced the curious sensation of pain fading swiftly into a pleasurable sense of wellbeing. It was as though she were being swept with some beam of healing, stimulating light. In fact, it stimulated her to a point that she knew was abnormal. So she opened her eyes.

She lay on the polished metal floor of a glass cage. Dimly, beyond its walls she heard and saw great machines working. A door opened, and a large man reached in and pulled her out, none too gently.

She was in a large room that looked like a cavern. It was filled with an array of gigantic machines whose purpose she could not have divined had her life depended on it. Indirect lighting came from somewhere, but she was not as concerned about such details as she was about the man who confronted her.

He was big, about the size of the Russian Major in Santa Cruz.   His hair was bright red and his face was heavily freckled, but deathly pale. His eyes were a faded brown. His lips were thick and rather indefinite in shape. Every line in his face was one that had been woven there by the cruel personality of a maniac.

He wore mediaeval type leggings and boots, a wide leather belt, and a leather jacket. This was open and sleeveless, revealing hairy chest and arms.

"Welcome home, my luscious, little pigeon," he said, in a hoarse voice. His eyes were obviously unaccustomed to subterfuge. He drank in her anatomy as pervertedly as possible.

"Where am I?" she demanded, strengthened by a maddening fear.

"Surface imbeciles have always referred to our blissful little Paradise as Hell," he said, drawing her close to him. "But we like it. Maybe you could learn to like it, too."

He tried to kiss her, but she struck him as she had Nicholas the First, this time making full use of her ring. It tore a bloody gash in him. But she suddenly found out that she was not dealing with a human being, not even an insane human, for this creature was a true fiend of Hell.

His eyes reddened with madness. In his throat rumbled a bestial growl, while his hands curled like talons. He came at her as the personification of murder, teeth bared back inhumanly in evident readiness to rend her throat apart. She felt as though she was shriveling in withering horror, paralyzed, rooted to the spot. It all happened like a flash of lightning, from the instant that she struck him. His iron hard hands grabbed her arms, bruising flesh and bone. His bared fangs struck her throat with battering ram force. While her senses reeled in a maelstrom of intangible terrors and pain she heard shouting and running feet, and she felt other hands grasp her. Scuffling and physical combat buffeted her about, followed by a sudden calm.

Groggily, painfully, she focussed her eyes upon the scene

before her. She still stood, though weakly, in the middle of the room, her clothes half-torn from her body, the feverish warmth of blood on her neck and breast. She sobbed hysterically as she glanced about her.

The madman lay before her on the floor, stone dead. Three men were bent over him, studying him. They were dressed somewhat the same as he, but were slighter of build. When they looked up at her she saw that they were as capable of running berserk as the first one had been.

"How did you kill Larson?" they asked her. Their eyes roamed over her body. "You have no visible weapons."

"I—did not—kill him," she stammered back. "Please get me out of this place." she groaned, sobbing in horror.

"This woman must be Lillian Germain," said one of them, getting to his feet. "It's that damned husband of hers. Yodi said they dis-rayed Germain at Santa Cruz, but he must have tricked the ray somehow. He's still alive. He killed Larson! He said he'd kill anybody who harmed her. You'd better call Yodi. He'll know what to do. And go get some bandages. The dame's bleeding." The little fiend looked at her closely. He reached out a hand to pluck at her tattered blouse, then changed his mind, somewhat fearfully.

Yes darling, I am with you. Lillian suddenly sensed the welcome thought of her husband. *You are in mortal danger. I am sorry there is no time to enlighten you, but you have been brought into the lair of Earth's greatest enemy, which is equivalent to Hell itself. There is so little time. All I can do now, dearest, is to establish the fact among them that to touch you is to die. But there is other work I must do after that. Until we can get you out of there with impunity I will have to leave you on your own for a short space of—*

Lillian covered her face with her hands and cried out, "Oh, Stephen! Don't leave me! Don't leave me! For the love of God take me from this place!"

HAD she not been on the verge of shell shock before this whole new experience under ground, she might have faced her predicament with greater courage, but now there was little resilience left to her mind and spirit. Had it not been for Germain's message to her she would have collapsed completely.

Take it easy now, Germain warned her. *These are madmen, all of them. Try not to antagonize them.*

Just when one of the fiends had finished applying a light bandage to her, there stepped into the room a shriveled little ghoul in a monk's habit. His face was of an indefinable clayish complexion and texture, his bulbous eyes sickly blue and watery. These latter were fixed intently upon Lillian's eyes as he approached her.

"Yes," he answered one of the men who followed him. "This is Lillian Germain, I have seen her many times in the visi-screens. Her husband, no doubt, thinks that he can rob us of so delectable a fruit, but we may be able to fool him. Woman, you must follow me," he said. "Just remember that your loving husband cannot kill everybody around here. We have an unlimited number of slaves to work the ray machines, and they can kill you or shock you, with unimaginable pain, at will. So obey me…"

Lillian, dazedly trying to remember Germain's advice, followed the hideous dwarf-monk unwillingly. They walked through great stone passageways, some of them darker or brighter than others, many of them half-filled with frightening shadows. She had the vague impression that these caves and corridors were practically endless. Exactly where she was, who these mad people were, or who had built these mighty caverns or why, she did not know, but she felt that whoever lived here now had usurped the ancient abode of a far superior type of people. For she saw at intervals great carvings or monuments, which revealed marvelous gigantic beings with god-like faces, filled with calm benevolence and wisdom. Another thing she sensed was an air of very extreme antiquity about everything, as though these great halls had been made in times so far past as to be beyond the range of imagination.

The little ghoul led her to a large opening, which was a door on one side of the passage, yet, which looked like the facade of a great building. She walked up a number of large, age-worn steps with him before entering this place, followed by the other, three men.

"This," explained Yodi, "is the most important spot either in or upon the Earth, for here rules ancient *Kar,* Emperor of all nations."

She found herself in a gigantic foyer of some kind supported by a vast circle of gargantuan pillars, Mayan type columns composed of the solid rock. They were carved beautifully to represent, allegorically, the history of a wondrous race of people. The benevolently smiling faces of these silent statues fascinated her and made her wonder, in the midst of her apprehension, who these people might have been in ages past. The floor was a mosaic work in marble and crystals of rock. A huge fountain still splashed water in the center of the foyer.

Beyond, they entered the interior of a great subterranean palace. They crossed circular corridors and passed through great halls that were filled with wonderful machines and devilish looking people. And finally they arrived in a large throne room. Several men on the circular stairs leading to the throne turned and stared at her with unconcealed desire.

When she saw what was on the throne she stopped suddenly, as though someone had frozen her to the floor. There sat Kar, "Emperor of all nations," and King of the Ghouls, if there ever was one. He was a big man, perhaps it might be said that he was of abnormal or inhuman proportions, and he was dressed in a black monk's habit. His complexion was like clay and his flesh was lumpy. His eyes were bulbous and watery and red-rimmed like cups of blood. His whole face seemed to sag into wrinkles like that of an ancient St. Bernard dog, weighted down by the heaviness of his huge lower lip and gluttonous jowls. Some affliction caused him to breathe only through his nose, which made it necessary for the latter to be always agape. Always it was half obscured by a drooping tongue, and his lower lip was apparently incessantly moist with drool.

Kar was incredibly ancient looking, as though he had been living for centuries on stimulants alone.

"Come here, my child," he said, in a deep wheezy voice. He lifted a great, chapped looking clayish hand and beckoned to her.

The room was so silent now that she could swear everyone was listening to her heartbeat. She could only look back at that living nightmare on the throne, but she could not move.

Then Lillian was subjected to the ancient pain ray by a hidden operator. The jolt was not as powerful as the one which Germain had experienced in Santa Cruz, but it was enough to make her lose all color, to clench her fists until her nails pierced her palms, and then to scream until in one instant she became hoarse.

AS QUICKLY as the ray had struck her it was taken from her, and she staggered, almost falling. Her eyes only widened in terror as she looked up at the man on the throne, while she trembled from the after effects of the momentary torture. It had been a pain so great that she thought secretly they might be able to force her to do anything under the threat of it. That is, she *thought* that she thought secretly, but the telepathic ray sentinels could read her mind and transfer the thoughts to Kar.

"Now let us see," wheezed the latter. "For your stubbornness in not doing as I ordered you to do you have had to be taught a lesson by means of a pain ray treatment, a telaug ray sentinel was just killed by your husband, and no doubt your husband has been put to some pains in his efforts to make good his threats." The ugly ghoul raised his eyebrows. "I should think it far more economical and practical, in the long run, to be obedient. After all, your husband no doubt has other things to do in this world besides looking after you. Think how selfish you are, demanding his attention like this when he is probably needed elsewhere."

The fiend! came Germain's thought to Lillian. *He knows just where to strike you!*

But it's true, darling—she thought back. You may love me, yes, but I said you were too much of a god to worry about a mortal woman like me. I was terribly frightened and upset for a while because of all I've been through, but I'll face anything—even this Hell, itself—before being responsible for your being distracted from the much greater work for which you must be needed. Don't consider me, darling. Consider the world.

The ghoul on the throne took advantage of this psychic intercourse to communicate mentally over the telaug beam to his chief ray guard.

You've got to find a way of killing Germain!—he thought.

The mechs have not been set in twenty thousand years for such a high mentality as his—complained the ray man. He is above our range. Unfortunately, we don't know enough about these mechs to adjust them to the higher frequencies.

Then determine where he is and kill him with dis-ray!

That is difficult, since his thoughts are not being transmitted on a beam. He, himself, is here in disembodied form.

Then there is no way?

We're still trying.

I hold a high reward for the man who can find and destroy Germain's mind and body.

What reward is that?

His wife…naked as an egg.

Karthen grinned nauseatingly at Lillian. "Will you step forward?" he said.

Without a word, she did as she was told. However, on the first step of the dais she hesitated, overcome again by the horror of the man's countenance.

"Very well," he said. "Now I will tell you why you are here. First, as a hostage to put your husband on his good behavior. Secondly, to pay back a few debts we owe him for some killing of our people in the Machu Picchu area of Southern Peru, recently. Thirdly, we always need new blood in our veins to keep us from getting troglodytic. We should like to have you be one of us, my dear." He saw the revulsion in her face.

"Do not be deceived," he continued, "into believing that we are so bad or unprincipled. Here we live longer and learn more than surface men. We also fear for our existence at their barbaric hands, because we feel that their blundering science may at any time stumble upon certain discoveries, such as atomic energy, for example, which may constitute a real threat to us. So we prepare ever to defend ourselves.

"You may also wonder why we prefer the caverns to the surface world. This is because the sun's rays are poisonous. They are the chief cause of your mortality on the surface. Down here we live by artificial rays which are more beneficial, although I must admit that the machines which produce such rays have deteriorated to the point where even their own emanations are becoming contaminated with radioactivity. Radioactivity is the Enemy Number One of all life. That is why the Elder Race sought out a home beyond the stars—in eternal darkness where the tides of integration, are only beginning."

LILLIAN'S eyes were wide with puzzlement and wonderment, in spite of her predicament, and in spite of the hellish ugliness of Kar's face.

"There is much of knowledge which may be given to you here," he continued, "of ancient and wondrous things entirely beyond the ken of surface Man. So really your imprisonment here with us will not be as bad as you think—*if* you care to cooperate without our having to mould your mind under the influence of the ro mechs."

Don't ever let him convince you of his sincerity, warned Germain. *I've just examined his rotten soul, and I see there is no need for Satan here, Lil. You're looking at his number one stand in. This man has lived here in these caverns for five centuries and has knitted all the major cavern centers of Earth into a sort of satanic empire, on a pattern established by various long-lived predecessors. By means of the ancient machinery left behind by a certain race of god-like men who once lived here in times beyond memory, Kar and his minions have succeeded in keeping very much alive the old legend of Hell. In fact, what they maintain here is the actual Pit. So don't ever—*

Stephen—Lillian interrupted him with her own thought. If you love me or if you cherish my own love for you, then please, in the name of Heaven, forget me. Nicholas the First is a heavenly cherub beside this fiend, and if this is an example of what you have to fight, then you are not going to have any time for me. I can realize the nature of my personal sacrifice in this matter, darling, when I beg you to do this, but it is little enough to do in the face of what is threatening everybody at the hands of these ghouls. Please, in memory of our love, I beg you, dearest!

God bless you, Lil—replied Germain. *If I come through this fight and really succeed in what I am going to try, then you will hear from me again. If not, nothing will matter to any of us. Just remember, Lil, if I'm a god, as you call me, I've only got one angel, and that's you. So long, sweetheart!*

"Stephen!" Lillian cried aloud, while Kar observed her with a knowing leer. The cry had been involuntary, like the sound that a cord makes when it snaps. For Lillian knew that her great guardian angel was gone. She was alone in Hell.

But she was puzzled by a momentary expression of consternation that passed over Kar's ugly face. She did not know that Germain was working on him.

Remember this, Emperor of an anthill, he warned, wrathfully. *You can be snuffed out just as easily as the rest. I spare you only because you are appointed by me as my wife's custodian. I delegate you, because you have the highest authority to protect her. So if anybody harms her it's your fault. I shall return, and when I do I'll look for her. If I do not find her, or if I do find her and she has been so much as scratched, you will die as surely as you are Satan's bastard son!*

I am leaving now, but you may be interested to know that if I succeed in what I am going to attempt, your already worthless carcass will acquire a negative value. There will be no escape, unless you have taken proper care of my wife. Until we meet again, my little Caesar.

Kar's clay-like complexion darkened to purple. His bloody eyes blazed in maniacal fury. His callused giant's hands clenched and unclenched. Drool poured from his bloated lip and he seemed on the verge of apoplexy.

Steady, Kar—came the augmented thought of his chief ray guard. The latter played a mild soporific beam on him to calm him down—We can't catch Germain's thoughts on the telaug. What did he say?

Kar stood up, trembling with anger, and sweating profusely. He looked so inhuman that Lillian hid her face from him.

He staggered like a drunkard from the dais, down the steps, shouting hoarsely to all present attendants, and to Yodi in particular.

"A declaration of war has been made!" he shouted. "Germain must be in Agarthi. It is there that we must strike! Yodi, how soon can your ships be ready?"

Yodi's bulbous eyes gleamed enthusiasm. "In one month," he answered.

"It must be sooner," demanded Kar. "Call my council together. The time has come, men! The sands of the ages have run out the glass. Earth's time is at hand. I, Kar, shall rise out of the Earth and smite and destroy with the fire of the dis-ray, and I shall possess the entire globe. I am done with patience and waiting!"

Thus, some fifty millions of dero were set in motion as never before, the object being destruction, as usual, but this time in catastrophic proportions.

CHAPTER TWELVE
In the Abyss

GERMAIN sat in a comfortable, reclining chair. His head had healed, showing several great vertical scars. His cranium, as an end result of Borg's experiment, had been increased almost to twice its normal size, but otherwise he was in perfect condition.

He sat in a spacious, simply furnished room on top of the great palace of Agarthi. From his position he could look out over a balcony at all the beautiful city of that peaceful cavern in the heart of the Himalayas.

Before him sat a very old man dressed in a blue robe, the back of which was emblazoned with the customary Sword of Agarthi, but which was topped by a mystic symbol, the ancient star and crescent. This man's name was Mandir, and he was close to one thousand years of age. He was Agarthi's chief mystic, aside, of course, from the King of the World, himself.

The King of the World was also present at this meeting. He, too, was incredibly old, but the preserving methods of Agarthian science had worked much more successfully on him than they had on Mandir, who worked too hard and paid too little attention to his corporeal nature to give the doctors a chance. The King stood in the center of the room, listening to Germain and Mandir.

"Then you really feel," said Germain, "that to rescue my wife from Kar's hands by means of the teleportation apparatus would precipitate a war prematurely?"

"Yes," came Mandir's gentle, ancient voice. "You must realize that you have stirred the caverns with fear, because they have no known defense against you as they have against our various rays. They could even disrupt a teleportation beam, and the result might be a ghastly distortion of the person being transferred. But they cannot shield you out because they do not know how. Given proper strength and the right frequency, their fields could actually shield you out, but they are stupid in the face of variable factors. Be that as it may, they seem to recognize in you the symbolism of Agarthi, itself. When you anger them, you anger them against Agarthi. So, although it is certainly deeply regrettable that your wife is in their hands it is most advisable not to antagonize Kar at this time."

Germain thought for a long time, and in his secret thoughts he now felt guilty because of his last message to Kar. Then he said abruptly, "I must begin my journey at once, if possible."

The King of the World raised his eyebrows with new interest.

"Ah, then the deed of the prophecy involves a journey," he remarked.

"Yes," said Germain. "I have asked for the presence of both of you to give me some information."

"You have only to ask," said the King.

Old Mandir licked his lips and leaned forward eagerly. At last he would hear what deed it was that could save the world, as the prophecy had indicated. Many there were in Agarthi who could have read Germain's mind, if he had allowed them to, but none had attempted to invade the private world of his thoughts. Agarthians were like that.

Germain looked at his two friends calmly and said, *"Where are the Elder Gods?"*

NO ONE answered him. Mandir's mouth opened slightly in amazement and he looked wonderingly at the King. The latter's face had acquired suddenly the impassiveness of an Elder Race monolith. But his great eyes bored into Germain's.

At long last, he spoke. "You would contact the Elder Race?"

"Yes," said German. "Why not?"

The King sighed. He made a sign to Mandir to explain, which the latter did, almost disappointedly.

"In the first place," he began, slowly, "the Elder Race is composed of entities so superior to us that our appealing to them would be similar to the appeal of a dog to a man."

"Many a benevolent master has been moved by the entreaties of his dog," retorted Germain, somewhat displeased with Mandir's simile.

"True, because a dog's wants are fundamental and may be appreciated by higher intellects, but on the other hand—"

"What is more fundamental," interrupted Germain again, "than the survival of Humanity?"

"Well," smiled Mandir, "granting the possibility of making an appeal, which I still doubt, you must consider that the Elder Race has by this time achieved absolute immortality. For some of its number to return into this galaxy again it would mean subjection to relative mortality, because they would become contaminated with radioactivity in more or less degree, wherever the light rays of the older stars might reach them. This would be a great sacrifice, as one of those great beings is worth half of an Earthly nation in his wisdom and ability."

"We must not take too humble an attitude," admonished Germain. "For it must be remembered that we all represent potential Elders. If Earth's surface humanity is destroyed by the deros, the possibilities of a new future Elder Race will cease to exist. So I think that helping us out is worth the time and trouble of a goodly number of the present Elder Race.

"Moreover, ultimate wisdom is imperfect if not applicable. After all, selfishness is not a part of godliness. The sacred responsibility of a god, it seems to me, is to use his powers to the advantage of lesser beings."

"Well spoken," commented the King of the World, smiling his approval. "Perhaps you would be a good ambassador for Agarthi, Germain, but there are, beyond these considerations, further difficulties."

"The chief physical difficulty," broke in Mandir, "is distance."

"I am not thinking of one of your interstellar ships," put in Germain.

"I know. You are an adept at astral projection. But it is in this field that I can give you the most authoritative advice. Such projection is also limited."

"By what? The speed of light? I think not."

"No, it is not that. It is an almost inexplicable thing. It is the danger of having to go so swiftly that one loses his points of reference. You may become *lost.*"

Germain was somewhat impressed by this. The aspect of his astral self-wandering about in Infinity without a corporeal anchorage was not encouraging. But he had foreseen such dangers.

"Where," he repeated, slowly, "are the Elder Gods?"

"They live in the Darkness of Beginning, in the Distant Places," said the King of the World. "Such a journey, if possible, would endanger sanity, itself, even for your mind. Then, too, there are unknown laws of velocity to which even the astral body is subject."

"I'll chance that," said Germain. "But where are the 'Distant Places'; where is the 'Darkness of Beginning'?"

"Beyond the stars," said Mandir.

"Beyond the—?" Germain looked startled. "But I thought—"

"Your thought is correct. In the Finite there is an infinitude of units. The stars are endless, when taken in all, but each unit of the endless whole is a galaxy, a vast universe, a molecule. The distances between the galactic masses, or the universes, is unthinkable to our minds. The Elder Gods live somewhere on dark worlds outside any existent universe, in the dark abyss of Endlessness and Nothing."

"If I were to contact the Elder Race and convince some of their number to come to our aid, could they come to us *physically,* in time to help?" asked Germain. "That is, do they have any way of counteracting the laws of Relativity in their flight in order to surpass the speed of light physically? I'm thinking of Lorentz-Fitzgerald contraction and mass increase with velocity. Also inertia. If they could overcome that—"

"We do not know," replied the King of the World. "What you contemplate seems all impossible, even to me, but it is in the prophecy that you will do it. I suggest you explain how we can help you."

"By stimulator ray," answered Germain. "And by taking good care of my body while I am absent."

"This can be done," said the King.

"Then I start tonight."

FROM Panama to Havana, the armies and allies of Nicholas the First were winning the greatest war ever fought in recorded history, yet it all meant less than any had ever meant before, because a more powerful ruler was already deploying his forces underneath the surface of Earth to conquer that which was to fall to the conqueror.

But while all this was transpiring, an astral entity swept out onto the road of stars, bent upon the salvation of Humanity, itself. This was Germain, soaring much farther than he had ever ventured previously, and with a thought-augmented velocity that far surpassed light. When he traversed the dreaded line, which was the universal speed limit, he could no longer detect the presence of the stars. All he could do was plunge into the unknown, speed-induced blackness, not even sure that he was still a part of the same space-time continuum he had known. Already he was utterly lost, and he realized that his only salvation was a contact with the Elder Gods.

As he progressed in lonely emptiness he could not help but contemplate the immensity of the Cosmos and Man's limited perspective of it. Before surpassing light's velocity he had seen the flaming white cauldron of Creation and Destruction, suns aborning and waning without end, huge nebulae which could span a hundred solar systems, the vast plethora of light and matter which signified cosmic creation, and the black nebulae, funeral shrouds of half a universe of ancient suns. The sight and the experience almost stunned his consciousness and sent him reeling, spiritually blinded, into the Limbo of the Lost.

Here he had seen the great fundamental of life-energy that is vibration, vibration that is a surge between extremes. Upon twin opposites was the Cosmos built, and between them surged Existence, like the pendulum of a giant clock: Construction and Destruction; Light and Darkness; Matter and Void; Heat and Cold; Yesterday and Tomorrow; Infinity and Zero; Love and Hate; Peace and War; Riches and Poverty; Health and Sickness; Joy and Sorrow; Man and Woman; Life and Death. That was the secret of existence. Without the surge and striving between the two there would be no comparison, no relativeness, nothing. Conformity with this law of surge and strife was wellbeing, happiness. Nonconformity meant atrophy and death. The, greater the surge between extremes, the greater the falls into the negative opposites, the greater the rise toward the pinnacles of positive ecstasy. Therefore the answer to all happiness and to all life was striving, even though fundamental law pointed out that the inevitable end was to fall once more, only to begin again. The continuity of the action was Eternity, the Infinite. The inevitability of the repeated cycle was the Finite. Finite and

Infinite were one…

WHITHER MOVES THE THINKER OF THE ULTIMATE FUNDAMENTAL?

Germain was startled. His headlong acceleration ceased. His being had been almost obliterated by the vast power of the thought which had been cast at him. He slowed down, desperately, but he was moving far too fast to see the stars, if, indeed, he were still within the confines of the universe.

I seek that Elder Race of gods which left the planet known to them as Lemuria, he thought back, as powerfully as he could.

Was this his contact? Or had he stumbled upon alien entities of vast power who would act against him? There was no way of judging time in this endlessness. The ponderous pendulum of Eternity seemed to swing its course before an answer came.

US YOU HAVE FOUND BY YOUR COURAGE AND OUR WILLING GUIDANCE. YOU WOULD PETITION OUR HELP, AND WE READ IN YOUR SOUL THE REASON WHY.

Germain felt relieved that not much time would have to be wasted on explanations. They were aware of everything he had to tell them or ask them.

Then I have only to reiterate the question which I came to ask, he thought. *Can you, and will you, help us?*

Suddenly, he knew that he had slowed down within the limits of light's velocity. He saw not stars, but *universes…*

THE universes took the place of the firmament. They were, however, but ghostly lanterns hung on startling darkness, glimmering far away, as though light, itself, were dissipated in distance. This, at last, was the Darkness of Beginning. These incalculable interstices of endlessness were the soul-dizzying Distant Places in which lived the Elder Gods. Far ahead in blackness he was aware of a great dark world, lightless, motionless. *Home of the gods.* To this place he had just directed a question upon which hung the fate of four billion mortal beings, now lost on an invisible speck of matter behind a trillion, trillion stars. He hated himself for recognizing the comparative insignificance of his mission.

Yet, a great god-mind deigned to answer his stated question:

YES, it said. WE CAN. AND WE SHALL... RETURN WHENCE YOU CAME, TERRESTRIAL. OUR LAWS FORBID THE ENTRANCE OF STRANGERS AND LOWER INTELLECTS HERE. RETURN. AND IF YOU ARE LOST ON THE STAR ROAD WE SHALL GUIDE YOU, EVEN AS WE TRAVEL WITH YOU...

Germain, as he altered his astral course in an attempt to turn back, thought he heard the legendary music of the spheres accompanying a heavenly choir of giant angels. But it was only the music of elation coming from within his being...

CHAPTER THIRTEEN
The Eve of Armageddon

THE President of the United States spoke impatiently to his appointment secretary. "I can't see the man, no matter who he is," he exclaimed, looking distractedly at a neat little card on his crowded desk blotter.

The card said: "Major Michael Kent, representing Stephen Germain."

The tired President had a fond recollection of Germain. Although he could never, as a politician, openly subscribe to some of Germain's outspoken principles, nevertheless he had admired and envied the fellow's sharp social vision and his daring self-expression.

"Major Kent has been trying desperately to see you and everybody else for the past three days," explained the gray-haired male secretary. "He says it is imperative that you see him at once—a matter of world-shaking proportions, evidently. I explained to him of course that—"

"That everybody comes shaking the world at me, eh?" put in the president. "Well, it is shaking, we can't deny that. Tell me, whatever happened to this fellow Germain? Oh yes, yes, I remember. Some strange business about hypnotizing the Russians at Santa Cruz. An amazing thing that, almost unbelievable."

"Germain was reported as missing after that," said the secretary, "but Major Kent insists he is very much alive and that he has been in communication with him."

"Is that so? All right, then, let me see Major Kent. I'll count this interview as today's fifteen minute recess," he checked the recess off the days calendar and sat back in his chair, sleepless eyes closed, to wait for Kent.

Kent's furlough did not seem to be doing him much good. He had lost weight and anyone who looked at him could tell by his weary eyes that he had passed some sleepless nights lately.

He came up to the president's desk and saluted, however, with his one good arm, in best army tradition. "Thank you, Mr. President," he said. "You'll not regret this, I am sorry to have to appear melodramatic, but I bring a message to you from a place called Agarthi, and—"

"Won't you be seated?" said the president. "I called you in to ask you about Captain Germain. You say he is alive?"

"Yes, very much so," replied Kent, not accepting the offer to take a seat. He made a habitual gesture in an attempt to crack his knuckles, but this was no longer possible because of his withered hand, a result of Pavlovich's death ray.

"Look, Mr. President," he said nervously. "I'm sorry to be abrupt, but it's taken me three days to get to you. What is involved here probably took many tens of thousands of years to happen, and I've got only minutes to explain it. The points are these:

"Number One:—Things are going bad for Americans in the war, because it now looks definitely like the Russians are going to take over.

"Number Two:—If the Russians do take over it won't do *them* any good because a much more powerful enemy, unknown to you but backed by the most superior weapons on Earth, is going to overthrow Nicholas the First, even before the final phase of the war.

"Number Three:—If this latter enemy takes over, it will be curtains for Civilization. There would be nothing we could do about it. Their weapons could snuff us out before we knew what it was all about. This attack may occur at any moment.

"Number Four:—There is a place near Tibet called Agarthi. There the Agarthians have weapons and the disposition to help us, but they are too few to guarantee success.

"Number Five:—Stephen Germain has contacted someone who can help us out, but that someone must first talk to the entire world, to get them prepared for the biggest shakeup they've ever seen. This person is scheduled to go on the air from a radio television station in Agarthi at midnight tonight, Central Standard Time. What this person has to say will be the most important thing this world has ever heard in its history. As many people as possible should be listening in. It is Stephen Germain's personal request that you arrange a world wide hook-up, throughout what's left of the Democratic Nations, and to request emergency cooperation of Nicholas the First to allow the Russian World State nations to listen also…"

"Wait a minute," protested the president. "What kind of crazy folderol is this? Are you ill, Major Kent?" He rang for his secretary. "Major Kent," he said, standing up, impatiently, as the secretary hurried in, "I am a practical and a busy man. What you say is incredible and a bit too much for me to swallow. Good day!"

Several plainclothesmen hurried in to accompany Kent out. Kent turned back toward the president to have one last word.

"Sir, I am sorry as the devil to have caused a scene here, but I have only been following orders."

"Whose orders?" shouted the president, angered.

"Of Stephen Germain," replied Kent.

"Since when has he become your commanding officer?" retorted the president. "May I remind you, Major Kent, that this nation is still at war, and that your activities are at present subject to the long established regulations of the United States Army?"

Kent insisted. "You've got to make that radio television hook-up tonight or this will be the saddest day of your life."

"Take him away," said the president.

BUT that night, at 9:00 p.m. the president received confirmation from the office of International Televisor Communications that an unknown station in Inner Mongolia was insisting on the same thing. The station gave its location as Agarthi. G-men got Kent and began taking stock of the whole situation again, but everything they got out of their charge was so incredible that they finally decided he was shell-shocked.

Still, the president was bothered. Finally, he called his special aide on Communications. "Arrange," he said, "for the requested hook-up, as universal as we can make it. If we don't like what's being said we can censor it over here. If the thing's a fake, I'll utilize the time with a message of my own I've prepared on the war for my Fireside program. But you know I've been struck by this thing, somehow, more than I've cared to admit. I keep thinking of the strange incident at Santa Cruz. Now this Agarthi station appears on the air, corroborating at least a part of Kent's incredible story. I can't get out of my head, either, that famous Shaver mystery that occupied everybody's time so much a number of years ago. I've always wondered about that thing, and I remember something about this Agarthi place. It's all like a mad dream, on the one hand, but... Well, I know it's a risk of my own political neck, but there's something about this whole thing that strikes me squarely between the eyes. So arrange all the hook-ups you can and see how well the enemy will cooperate, at least the undergrounds, even if only out of curiosity."

The Communications aide whistled. "That's a large order, Mr. President, but we'll try our best. It's your baby and it's your neck..."

"Nicholas has a noose around it, anyway," muttered the president to himself. He sat down at his desk, synchronizing his watch with his desk clock. "Three more hours," he mused, "in which to enjoy my neck. Still, in these last days of American independence one might as well give anything a try…"

IF THE U. S. President could have seen what was going on just three miles underneath the capital building he might have begged Agarthi to start talking as soon as possible. And this thing that was going on below was merely a repetition of thousands of activities in similar centers located throughout the world. For the caverns of the ancients had been swiftly but strongly made, and they stretched in an interminable network almost everywhere.

Here beneath Chicago were great halls and chambers that had been enlarged by dis-ray machines in the past few decades, owing to the lucrative business which the deros were able to carry on here. They acquired slaves and provisions from the surface and were able to trade with such articles far and wide in the cavernous catacombs that led away from that center of activities.

And wherever the leading deros gathered, so did the ancient machines and weapons, in order to protect their holdings from competing centers, which, in spite of Kar's dictatorial unification, were liable to overthrow enforced fidelity in favor of an attractive gamble. Lined up under Chicago's surface arsenals and national military headquarters were huge dis-rays run by atomic energy, which latter was derived from hydrogen, split out of ordinary water from Lake Michigan, the basic fuel. These dissociator rays could cause matter to collapse into a nebulous mass of basic matter. They were powerful enough to dissolve Chicago by merely sweeping it like a broom. By shortening the effective distance of the beams they could open great pits in the Earth into which skyscrapers could fall and be buried. Or they could lengthen the effective distance and dissolve cubic miles of atmosphere, thus creating hurricanes. They also had atomic heat rays that could have raised Lake Michigan to the boiling point within a few days' time. And of course there were the terrible pain rays, and rays which could induce fever and produce most of the ailments and plagues in man which are attributable to the legendary unfilterable viruses, rays which could cause visions, nightmares and madness.

In other, greater caverns were gathering a number of marvelous, ancient ships of the void, giant wonder vessels built by the Elder Race when it was still young, still capable of entering the airless wilderness of interplanetary space, with loads of ray machinery and operators.

These could fly in or out of Earth's atmosphere, swifter than any bullet devised by man—even swifter than his fastest atom-bomb rockets. And just one of these ships would prove invincible to any and all terrestrial cities. But the dero had fully a hundred of them. Each one was equivalent in effective power and deadliness to anyone of Earth's surface navies. These were being prepared principally for the grand attack on Agarthi. The deros were prepared to spend ninety percent of that fleet, if necessary, to destroy Agarthi, its age-old enemy, and they were even quite confident that not fifty percent would be annihilated by Agarthi's giant dis-ray batteries before resistance would be burned through and smashed.

Most of the dero world was united by a mutual pact of organized distrust and fear, under Kar's typical domination. At his bidding, the dero attack would be unleashed. So sure was Kar of final triumph that he had arranged a special banquet, the festivities of which were to be dedicated to the celebration of dero victory and world mastery.

Delegates from all the principal caverns of the Earth had arrived, and it was expedient for Kar to impress them all for the sake of subterranean solidarity. So the banquet was probably one of the greatest known in all of dero history. It was the eve of the attack.

The banquet cavern was one that might have been reached by blasting through certain ancient concealed entrances as yet unfound by surface explorers in a certain well-known giant American cavern. It was a natural cavern, chosen especially for the occasion, because it was a quarter of a mile in length and half as wide and high. It had often been used for various important dero purposes, so it was well appointed with light, air, warmth, and ray machines.

Fully one thousand feet stretched the banquet table. It was fifty feet wide, as though it were the proscenium of the greatest theatre ever built. For days and weeks the crowds and provisions had gathered. Wines and sharper liquors, brought from everywhere, from Upsala to Mendoza, rare *hors d'ouvres* from Mosul, Constantinople, Moscow, Paris, New Orleans, whole barbecued beef and pork, roasted fowl and sweetmeats from the western United States—and slaves.

There was an army of slaves, of all colors, races, sizes, shapes and purposes. Musicians, dancers, wrestlers, swordsmen, headsmen, and chosen and manufactured harlots.

Fully a thousand of the important figures of the dero world sat at that table, while as many slaves served them and bemused them. Weird, erotic music accompanied by much naked dancing, drunken exhibitions of debauchery, and general gluttony—these were the keynotes of the celebration.

KAR sat at a raised table at one end of the main table, in feudalistic fashion, accompanied by some of the highest chiefs of the dero world, some, in fact, who had been his rivals for power but who feared him enough to side with him in this great venture which he had planned.

Rangus Melchor, particularly, had been a threatening competitor to Kar, and he still brought with him his old air of defiance. An ugly brute of a man with a great, fat face and a head matted with black curls, he bore the stamp of the cruel Caesars of ancient times. His bloody tactics had made him the master of all the caverns of central Europe, which were the best organized of all. He sat at Kar's left.

Melchor had come on Kar's order, more out of envious curiosity than out of a sense of allegiance. He had come mostly to seek out a flaw in Kar, whereby he might get a wedge into him and eventually break him, usurping his throne for himself. And Melchor found at least a minor flaw to start on. He had found something that Kar secretly feared— Stephen Germain. The story of Germain had gone swiftly through the caves, and all who came to the feast had heard about Lillian, and how Kar seemed to be afraid to harm her for fear of death at Germain's hands. Here, indeed, was a worthy theme for Melchor's fertile and versatile mind. There was one basic principle that he could use as a lethal weapon: In the caves, the fittest survived; to be weak was fatal.

As he sat beside the monstrous, drooling Kar his beady eyes searched through the vast crowd of revelers and slaves who might be American women. There were hundreds of these latter, of course, mostly acting under the coercion of the ray operators who ran the ro machines which molded their wills to conform to that of the operator, but among all these there seemed to be no *particular* woman.

"Where," he said to Kar, "is the famous American woman, Lillian Germain? I hear she is a rare plum. Are you saving her for plucking later?" Here he pointed significantly to a girl who had just been fiendishly tortured and thrown bodily into a great fountain of white wine in the center of the table. As she struggled in the liquid, her life's blood, pouring from hundreds of mortal cuts, deepened its color, while the revelers filled their glasses from overflow spouts around the fountain's lip.

"She will not be seen here tonight," replied Kar, in a heavy tone. His sickly, bloody eyes gazed enraptured upon the unfortunate girl who was dying in the wine fountain.

"Why not?" demanded Melchor.

"Because I said so," replied Kar.

"Ho! Ho!" laughed Melchor. "Afraid of Germain!"

Kar looked at him like gray death. "I fear no man," he said, hollowly.

"Then why not bring her out?" insisted Melchor. "I'd like to see her. Besides, if harm should come to her at my hands I'm the one who would reap the punishment, if any, and not you."

By this time, many another dero chief was listening, and Kar clenched his great hands in vexation. He took another long swallow of a fiery Persian wine, which was his favorite. "All right," he said. "Kar will give you a treat." A daring gamble was being planned in his mind. He had to keep up his own front here, yet he was practical enough to realize that Germain was a real threat to him. He called mentally to his ray guard.

Have her brought—he thought to the operator of the telaug—suitably prepared, but covered with at least a single dancing veil. Make her dance with the ro mech and pump this thought constantly into her mind. Her only salvation tonight is to smile and laugh. Everybody around her she will consider as beautiful and worthy of her caresses. But do not have her come near this table! I don't want Melchor's paws on her. He might go too far.

And so it was that at that stage of developments when everybody was drifting into complete abandonment to their degenerate senses and bloodlusts, Lillian was brought forward among them. Under the strong influence of the ro mech her will was not her own. She walked, talked and laughed as one hypnotized. Her milk white skin was not easily obscured by the one black veil which was supposed to conceal her body from the feasters. Instead, as she placed her shapely bare feet on the bloodied table and began to dance slowly up the gamut of revelers, the veil only enhanced her tall, smooth female charms to the point where all else was disregarded by her audience.

Melchor forgot even his food, which was unusual. Instead, he feasted his eyes with uninhibited passion and a growing fever of desire. Never had he seen such a raven cloud of hair. And those flashing emeralds that were her eyes! What juicy cherries—those luscious lips! Kar saw the other's hand tremble as he wiped his mouth, eyes never leaving the dancing figure for a second. And he frowned in mortified consternation as she danced more swiftly in their direction.

Keep her away from here—he ordered to his ray operator.

As Lillian began to retrace her steps, Melchor stood up drunkenly and shouted, "Come here, you wench!"

"Sit down, Melchor," said Kar. "She'll be here in time. Have another drink and enjoy yourself."

But Melchor had seen a woman that inspired all the maniacal demon lust of which he was capable. He got onto his chair and stepped onto the table, while Kar half rose to his feet. But the latter could not protest, because this was an old tradition.

Someone was supposed to pluck the plum and devour it. It was an expected part of the entertainment. In fact, it looked good from the cavern's political standpoint, especially. Kar was defying Germain and giving Melchor, his greatest rival, the choicest prize of the evening. But in a way, everybody could participate. It was an ancient, much cherished game.

KAR sat back in his chair, great beads of sweat on his slightly greening face. It's out of my hands now—he told his ray, I *tried* to save her, damn it!

Lillian, her face glowing with radiant life under the stim-ray, whirled and dipped and smiled in a maddening dance. The feasters devoured her. They cheered at the sight of Melchor on the tabletop. One offered his sword.

"Slice her tenderly with this," the maniac shouted, hysterically. "And then the fountain!" He pointed to the wine fountain where the other girl now floated, dead.

"Yeah, the fountain!" cried the crowd. "Cut her well so that all may drink her!"

First, they knew, Melchor would take her, to the entertainment of all, but so depraved was the crowd that bloodlust was even stronger than the other. Melchor did not take the sword. He knocked it aside and said, "Later."

When he was almost upon her, Lillian's own consciousness awoke to reality. This, too, was a part of the ancient procedure. Now that Kar had given up, the ray operator followed the dictates of tradition. He withdrew the ro mech control and left the victim on her own. The mental anguish was always more enjoyable to others that way.

Lillian was at once aware of her near nakedness, and she clung to her veil in abject mortification, mingled with incredulous amazement and abject horror. From Kar's pulpy face and the dead girl in the fountain to Melchor's obvious approach her eyes flew, taking in her situation in one brief moment.

Her first impulse was to scream, but then she suddenly remembered that she had promised herself to face Hell, even unto death, before flinching. She had known she would end in this place, so the sooner the better. After he was done with her they would put the sword to her, which was what she would want anyway.

Rangus Melchor was the object of all eyes as he reached Lillian and tore the veil from her body. Even Kar leaned forward at the sight of her, which was like a living white flame. Surprisingly, her head was up, eyes glaring proud defiance at them all. Melchor, nothing daunted, drew her greedily into his fat arms...

Blam!

The crowd was on its feet, a thousand mouths dropping agape. For Lillian had disappeared into thin air, and the passionate Melchor now lay pinned squarely to the table by a giant, golden sword!

Kar's clayish face turned pale for the first time in five centuries. "The Sword of Agarthi!" he exclaimed.

Deathly silence pervaded the cavern. Then, all eyes turned toward their leader. Kar's clayish color returned. His eyes began to blaze with the old fire of rage. His shapeless mouth struggled into an exultant grin.

"They've asked for it," he shouted. "Let the attack begin! Get to your posts and communication points. All chiefs take over your commands. Your ships must leave for Agarthi within the hour. Before the sun rises, Agarthi must be blasted from the Earth. Then turn upon all the nations and destroy them. Go!"

At his commands, pandemonium broke loose. The cave emptied so fast that no one noticed what direction Kar finally took. None there were alive, in fact, who knew of his secret exit...

CHAPTER FOURTEEN
When a God Spoke

WHEN Lillian Germain materialized in the receiving chamber of the teletransporter at Agarthi, a voluminous cloak was immediately placed about her by several Agarthian scientists and she was given a pair of warm, fur-lined slippers. But she had no eyes for those things, no time to think of where she was, for there before her, his head's size camouflaged by a thin turban, was her husband.

The transition from Hell to this comparative Heaven broken down all inhibitions. She ran to him without the slightest ceremony and flung herself crying into his arms.

Neither the scientists nor the gathered Agarthian citizens denied them privacy at that moment. They all turned to the televisor screens and watched the scenes transpiring in the dero caverns. A great tenseness and expectancy was in the air.

"My darling..." said Germain. "Sometimes it seems that life crawls through a hole too narrow for the broad shoulders of Hope. This moment is something I had long since given up as an impossibility. But here you are, like a faithful, homing angel. Thank heavens, Lil. All I can say is thank heaven. Yes, in spite of the actual existence of the lesser gods, such things as this make me revere a greater, single entity."

Lillian knew she should be asking a million questions, but she was content to merely relax in his arms, sobbing helplessly.

"This is Agarthi," said Germain. "It is the home of a wonderful people who are the feared enemies of the cave dero. We have all just declared war on the caves, Lil. Do you know what that means?"

"But—" Lillian began to shake herself mentally back into

reality. "How can this small place stand up against them? They are many and possess endless numbers of weapons."

Germain smiled proudly, and in his eyes she saw a starry sort of inspiration, as though he had just returned from the gates of Eternity. He led her up a pathway, through a rocky corridor.

"I would not trouble you now, sweetheart," he said, "were it not for the fact that something is about to happen which is more important than anything that ever happened before."

When they had reached a certain level, they turned into another passage and seemed to head straight for an opening in the side of the mountain. Soon they came into a room that looked like the bridge of a ship. Several people were there, gathered around a televisor apparatus. Germain led Lillian to a great stone balcony.

At first she drew back, involuntarily. Below the balcony was sheer nothingness. It was night, and the Earth far below was not visible. Above blazed a dazzling stellar spectacle— the clear night sky of the Himalayas.

"Look," said Germain, and he pointed into the darkness below.

Gradually, she began to make out what seemed to be the lights of a vast city. It seemed to be built on a great mound that stretched several miles in either direction.

"What is it?" she asked.

"It is not a city," said Germain. "It is a *ship*."

"A ship!" she exclaimed. "But that thing is miles—"

"Yes," said Germain. "Four miles long. It is a great battleship of the Elder Race, returned out of the Distant Places to give us a hand. And there's a whole armada of them floating upstairs, about one thousand miles out. Boy! Are the dero in for some surprises tonight. And is the *world*. Tonight, my darling, in about one minute from now, you are going to hear and see a *god,* right there on that televisor!

"A god?"

"Yes…those great beings in that ship out there are benevolent gods, so superior to us that we are specifically, only apes beside them. They are fully as godly as any ancient Zeus or Wotan or Thor, and their 'lightning bolts' will prove it."

"But how did they come here?" queried Lillian, overcome with amazement.

Germain looked pleased with himself. "I recruited them," he said. "They're great fellows—scare me to death every time I communicate with them."

"Scare *you?* Oh, Stephen, what's going on is too much for a person to grasp!"

"It's Armageddon," said Germain, "with a world-wide television hook-up. Even the Russians are going to see it."

"Shhh," admonished the televisor operator as the receiver came to life.

"This is it," said Germain, drawing Lillian closer to him…

IN CHICAGO, the President of the United States sat in the Senate Chamber, surrounded by a hundred men of state and as many news reporters. There, too, in a ring of G-men, sat Michael Kent, who watched keenly the developments on a giant televisor screen which had been hooked up for the emergency. It was midnight, but eighty percent of those present were quite skeptical about the validity of the place called Agarthi. They expected to witness a colossal farce.

A mysterious announcer, who would not show his face, began the ceremonies.

"People of the world!" he said. "People of all Earthly nations, of all races and creeds! The time of which legend and prophecy speaks has arrived. A thousand aged prophecies will be seen to prove themselves this night. This moment is second only to Judgment Day, itself, for you are on the verge of Armageddon!"

"Oh my gawd," snorted one U. S. senator. "It's one of *those* outfits. Throw the guy a quarter and turn him off."

"America," continued the announcer, "the one honest land where the doctrine of individual liberty has been adhered to, finds itself in this hour upon the verge of subjugation to Nicholas the First. But where is Nicholas the First?"

Reporters now pricked up their ears. The senator who had first protested looked disgruntledly at the representative from Louisiana. The latter raised bushy eyebrows, questioningly.

"Nicholas the First," said the announcer, "has fled. He has deserted his own men. At this moment he is traveling in a ship of space, out into the dreaded cold of the void—to escape *what?*"

The voice sounded somehow too authoritative, too confidently informed to really laugh at. Reporters began to scribble wildly. G-men looked at Kent, remembered his story, and muttered, "Well I'll be damned."

The president shushed his startled companions to silence and listened intently.

"What is Nicholas the First afraid of?" cried the voice of the announcer. "He is afraid of the *dero!* And what are the dero? To explain them simply, they are the living demons of Hell. Tonight they are going to attack the surface world. But first they attack Agarthi.

"Agarthi for ages has been the last hope for Mankind. The men of Agarthi alone have stood against the dero and held them in check, but now, without certain special help from an outside source, even we of Agarthi could be overcome by the great forces which the dero have swiftly prepared. That help consist of god-men of the Elder Race which first built Paradise on Earth. These benevolent beings come from the unthinkable depths of extra-galactic space at a time when we would all be utterly destroyed without their help. You should thank the God you worship that these Elders have condescended to take pity on us, because otherwise the dero would wipe us out.

"We have information that the dero plan to attack Agarthi in approximately one hour. Much of this battle you may be able to witness. But in the meantime, it is my incalculable honor to introduce to the world no less a personage than Rama Khan Tor, who is as great a living god as was Zeus, himself. This will be self-evident. Bless the world with your voice, o Rama Khan Tor!"

The President of the United States stared as one petrified at the screen, as did all the senators. The reporters, a hardier group where great news was concerned, continued to scribble madly, cigarettes and cigars long since dropped on the floor and forgotten. Photographers hysterically rattled their equipment to get it in readiness. Kent leaned slightly forward, eyes intent upon the televisor screen.

BEFORE sound there came a vision. Softly and slowly it swirled into shape. And soon the eyes of the world looked upon the vast, colorless face of Rama Khan Tor. It was the living face of a giant Buddha, eyes large, deep, and infinitely wise. Such miraculous strength was there in that perfect countenance that no mortal man could doubt that this was a being far superior to the ordinary *Homo sapiens*. It simply had to belong to a god, that beautiful, terrible giant's face. But if the face did, even more so the voice.

It was a voice that spoke an ancient mother language, which all listeners throughout the world seemed to be capable of understanding. But later it was suspected that some mass telepathy was also connected with that miracle. It was a voice that permitted no doubt. Its very sound penetrated to the spirit and commanded belief.

"TERRESTRIALS," said the god-voice, with infinite calm, "YOU HAVE LEARNED TOO SLOWLY AND THEREFORE YOU DESERVE THE ANNIHILATION WHICH THE DERO PLAN TO ADMINISTER THIS NIGHT. YET WE OF THE ELDER RACE TOOK PITY ON YOU AND HAVE MOVED TO SAVE YOU. AFTER ONCE DOING THIS THING WE SHALL NEVER REPEAT IT. ONCE YOU ARE OUT OF DANGER YOUR DESTINY WILL BE IN YOUR OWN HANDS, EXCEPT THAT WE SHALL LEAVE ONE HERE IN CHARGE WHO WILL GUIDE YOU. EVEN SO, WHETHER YOU DIE BY THE END RESULT OF YOUR OWN IGNORANCE, STUBBORNNESS AND VANITY OR WHETHER YOU LIVE TO BECOME ELDERS SUCH AS OURSELVES WILL DEPEND LARGELY ON YOUR FUTURE SELF-CONDUCT.

"ADMONITIONS TO YOU TERRESTRIALS ARE NOT SUFFICIENT TO GUIDE YOU. YOU MUST BE SHOWN THE WAY. THEREFORE IT IS THIS: VANITY IS IGNORANCE; HUMBLENESS IS WISDOM. FOR THIS REASON IT WAS ONCE SAID BY A GREAT GOD-SPIRIT WHO VISITED YOU TWO MILLENNIUMS AGO: THE MEEK SHALL INHERIT THE EARTH. ONLY THROUGH A HUMBLE APPROACH TO INFINITE KNOWLEDGE OF ALL THINGS IN SPACE AND TIME CAN YOU PROGRESS. DO NOT, EVER AGAIN, ATTEMPT TO REDUCE THE MIGHTY UNKNOWN DOWN TO THE STATURE OF YOUR FINITE AND ERRONEOUS UNDERSTANDING. DO NOT ATTEMPT IN VANITY TO REDUCE THE COSMOS, FOR THIS IS AN IMPOSSIBILITY; IT IS ONLY SELF-DECEPTION. INSTEAD, OPEN YOUR MINDS AND SPIRIT IN HUMBLENESS AND YOU WILL BECOME WISE. THE

SALVATION OF YOUR KIND IS IN BENEVOLENT WISDOM.

"FROM THIS DAY FORWARD, TERRESTRIAL MAN MUST ENTER INTO THE THIRD BASIC STAGE OF HIS DEVELOPMENT, OR ELSE IT WILL BE FOREVER TOO LATE. FOR ALMOST A MILLION YEARS, HOMO SAPIENS WAS ANIMAL, LIVING FROM DAY TO DAY EVEN AS THE LOWLIEST AMOEBA OR LICHEN, MERELY SEEKING HIS FOOD, HIS DRINK, HIS REST AND WARMTH AND PROCREATION. EVEN IN THE SECOND STAGE, WHEN HE BEGAN TO THINK IN THE ABSTRACT, WHEN HE BECAME A TRUE MAN AND BUILT FOR HIMSELF MIGHTY CIVILIZATIONS, REACHING EVEN INTO THE ELECTRONIC AND ATOMIC ERAS, HE STILL DEVOTED THE MAJOR PORTION OF HIS TIME AND ENERGY TO THE ACQUISITION OF THE PRIME NECESSITIES: FOOD, CLOTHING, SHELTER, PROCREATION. THERE WAS STILL NO GRACEFUL PERIOD OF LEISURE FOR UNTRAMMELED THOUGHT. IN IGNORANCE HE STILL SHORTENED HIS LIFE WITH FAULTY DIET AND DRUGS, WITH ACCELERATED LIVING AND OPEN EXPOSURE TO THE SUN'S DETRIMENTAL RAYS AND TO THE RADIOACTIVITY OF AIR, FOOD, AND WATER. LIFE IS STILL TOO SHORT FOR THE ACQUISITION OF MASS WISDOM. YOU DIE AS ADOLESCENTS, OFTEN IN THE AWFUL STENCH AND FIRE OF CARNAGE AND DESTRUCTION, WROUGHT BY CHILDREN WHO KNOW NOT WHAT THEY DO, OR PRECIPITATED UPON YOU BY EVIL ONES AGAINST WHOM YOU HAVE PREPARED NO DEFENSE.

"MAN MUST ENTER THE THIRD STAGE. AT

FIRST HE WAS ANIMAL. SECONDLY, HE TRIED, AT LEAST, TO APPLY KNOWLEDGE TO THE SOLUTION OF HIS PROBLEMS. AND HE BECAME, WEAKLY, WHAT MUST BE CALLED SCIENTIFIC. NOW MAN MUST BECOME MENTAL. HE MUST TAKE A GREAT STRIDE FORWARD; AS A WHOLE SPECIES HE MUST MUTATE, THROUGH THE APPLICATION OF LEISURE AND UNDER THE GUIDANCE OF WISDOM. IT WILL CONSTITUTE A GREAT STRIDE FORWARD TOWARD GODLINESS. WHICH IS YOUR GOAL. THIS IS WRITTEN IN NATURAL LAW.

"BUT YOU TERRESTRIALS ARE INCAPABLE OF TAKING THAT GREAT STRIDE FORWARD WITHOUT POSITIVE GUIDANCE FROM A HIGHER SOURCE. THE IGNORANT MASSES OF EARTH ARE TOO MUCH FOR YOUR MORE ADVANCED NATIONS TO CONTROL. WHEREAS THE MOST IGNORANT GROUPS, WITH THE SHORTEST AVERAGE LIFE SPAN, BREED THE MOST PROLIFICALLY, THE HIGHEST INTELLECTUALS AMONG YOU PRODUCE FEW CHILDREN, OR NONE AT ALL. YET THE FEW CHILDREN WHO ARE BORN TO THE INTELLECTUALS HAVE A CHANCE OF LIVING MUCH LONGER, EVEN OF ACQUIRING WISDOM. THE END RESULT IS A CONDITION WHERE IGNORANT BILLIONS OF HUMANS MUST DEPEND, FOR THEIR SALVATION, UPON THE LEADERSHIP OF AN INTELLECTUAL ARISTOCRACY. THE TIME WILL COME WHEN ALL MEN MAY WALK WITH EQUAL KNOWLEDGE. BUT IN THIS PARTICULAR STAGE, WHICH IS VERY PRECARIOUS, YOU REQUIRE THE GUIDANCE AND THE FIRM RULERSHIP OF A BENEVOLENT PERSON

WHO IS WISER THAN ALL OF YOU.

"IN ONLY A FEW MOMENTS YOU WILL WITNESS THE ATTACK OF THE DEROS UPON AGARTHI. YOU WILL SEE THE TYPE OF DEMON ENEMY WITH WHICH YOU WOULD HAVE HAD TO CONTEND DIRECTLY WERE IT NOT FOR AGARTHI. WE SHALL HELP AGARTHI TO SMITE THESE MANIACAL CREATURES AND ELIMINATE THEM TO THE LAST MAN, SO THAT THE ORDINARY TERRESTRIAL WILL HAVE NO EXCUSE, THENCEFORTH, TO FALL INTO THE WAYS OF VOLUNTARY EVIL.

"IN ORDER TO MAKE SURE THAT MANKIND WILL HAVE A GOOD OPPORTUNITY TO BENEFIT BY WHAT THE ELDER RACE DOES THIS NIGHT, WE SHALL, IN SOME MEASURE, GUARANTEE THE LASTING BENEFITS OF THIS BATTLE WHICH YOUR WRITTEN PROPHECIES REFER TO AS ARMAGEDDON. WE TAKE THE JUSTIFIABLE LIBERTY OF PLACING OUR CHOSEN DEPUTY IN CHARGE OF EARTH. ONE YEAR FROM THIS DATE HE WILL TAKE OVER ALL GOVERNMENT OF THE PLANET. THIS MAN IS THE LEADER OF AGARTHI, AND ON THE STRENGTH OF WRITTEN PROPHECY HE IS ALREADY CALLED THE KING OF THE WORLD. HE WILL RULE BENEVOLENTLY AND IN WISDOM FOR A THOUSAND YEARS, I, RAMA KHAN TOR, HAVE SPOKEN."

AS MYSTERIOUSLY as the vision had formed on the screen, it faded. There was a tendency in the U. S. Senate Chamber toward wild-eyed discussion. As one body, the audience there gathered began to argue and shout.

"That's a fake!"

"No, by Gosh, I believe it."

"It's over my head."

"Hey, George! Now you can payoff that bet! You said this was going to be the announcement of American surrender. Wow. Were *you* off the beam!"

"What a night," cried a reporter, knocking over a starry-eyed photographer. "Gang way for the telephone! Hold the presses!"

Some there were who merely sat and stared pensively at the blank televisor screen. Something of that ponderous speech had struck deeply into the more sensitive personalities, striking home at instincts and wondrous words of prophecy which they had heard in childhood, a remembrance when they were humble and had ideals—ideals which they were forced to sacrifice upon the altar of maturity.

These latter, such as Kent and the president, were the first to stand up and shout for silence when the televisor screen again became active...

"Ladies and gentlemen," said the unseen announcer at Agarthi. "This is Armageddon. It is a dangerous moment for all the world, but that danger is minimized by the existence of Agarthi, and by the presence of the Elder Race armada. The dero, who number some fifty millions and who have a hundred very deadly spaceships laden with weapons which the Elder Race itself once fashioned, are now well aware of their own danger. But, realizing that they will be given no quarter, they are out to fight to death. We of Agarthi hope that this sight will humble Man on Earth to the realization that he has yet very much to learn."

CHAPTER FIFTEEN
Finale

NICHOLAS THE FIRST did not know about the advent of the Elder Gods. He only knew that the dero were planning to take over. And that was enough.

The spaceship had been built behind the Urals in one month's time, through the utilization of all the greatest facilities of a powerful Russian industry. Steel plants, ship builders, radiotronic experts, all had been mobilized under seal of secrecy, fooled into believing that the ship was for Russian defense. It was a fine ship, large enough to carry tons of provisions and a crew of fifty men.

Nicholas, owing to commitments made necessary by the peculiar nature of the enterprise, had rewarded his cooperators either with a radium bullet or with passage on board the ship. He ended up with ten people, including the persistent Pavlovich. Dr. Borg he had not seen or heard from, so he had presumed, with some relief, that the scientist had not been able to prepare a similar vessel anywhere.

So it was that the spaceship took off on a supposed trial run, but provisioned secretly to make a trip to Mars. Nicholas knew there was sufficient atmosphere there to sustain life, especially within the ship after their oxygen supply ran out, because it could be supercharged with oxygen from a much thinner atmosphere than that which Mars would afford them. And, knowing of the presence of plant life there, he also assumed that animal life was also a necessary link in the biological cycle. The indisputable evidence of the canals, revealed clearly in 1957 by the first electronic telescope, meant that a highly intelligent type of beings lived there. These he was interested in recruiting to the cause of domination over the deros and the entire, solar system.

But first there was Agarthi. Nicholas felt that he should

deal with at least one potential enemy before leaving. To this purpose, he carried five powerful atomic bombs under the hull. They were held on by magnetic attraction only.

As the spaceship lifted up out of Russia and headed for Inner Mongolia, Nicholas the First bent anxiously over Pavlovich's shoulders to look at his radar screen, because Pavlovich was acting as bombardier.

"We're out of Earth's atmosphere," announced Pavlovich, elatedly. "Altitude, seven hundred and fifty-eight kilometers. Velocity: three thousand kilometers per hour. We'll have to circle until I plant the eggs."

The "eggs" were the bombs, which were to be radio controlled to their target. Svenga, the dark-skinned Russian mystic, had come along. He alone had mapped out the exact location of Agarthi. He stood also behind Pavlovich and watched.

"These bombs," he asked, "are completely capable of putting an end to Agarthi?"

"They are special," said Nicholas. "Beyond ordinance limitations for percentage of efficiency. They might even set up a chain reaction. According to calculation, one of them should be enough. But just to be sure, we'll throw all five at them."

"Always the safety factor," remarked Svenga, wryly.

"We are over Mongolia," announced Pavlovich. "Here go the bombs. One away..." His fat hand flipped a toggle switch, and at the same time he clamped a pair of receivers on his head and adjusted the remote controls on the first bomb.

They saw a black rocket shape dive into the field of vision of the radar.

"Two away..." And another sprang out toward Agarthi. The passengers on board braced themselves as the fast ship began to run a curved course over that part of Asia.

"Three away…"

"How soon will we see the explosion?" queried Nicholas.

"In about ten minutes for number one," said Pavlovich gleefully. "Four away…Five away… A kiss for you, Agarthi."

Not far above them floated a vast ship of the Elder Race. Its observers had easily detected the comparatively tiny ship and the ray operators had read the puny mind of each individual on board.

"I RECOGNIZE IN NICHOLAS THE ROOTS OF AN EVIL GENIUS," remarked one of the Elders. "HE SHOULD BE MADE TO SUFFER."

"THIS CAN BE DONE EASILY," smiled another Elder. "SHALL I SHOW YOU HOW?"

"YES, GHOSTUN DRA NOR. WE WOULD SEE IT DONE."

"SO BE IT," said the vast god-giant who was called Ghostun Dra Nor. And he began to arrange a just fate for all those who were on board the Russian ship.

First, Pavlovich's bomb control unit burned out. Secondly, the rocket bombs turned in their courses and headed back toward the ship. But if the terrified observers within had expected instant death they were deceived. Instead of colliding with the ship, the bombs began to circle it in ever narrowing orbits.

Nicholas shouted for full speed. The ship leaped far into space, throwing them all to the floor with the acceleration. But the whirling bombs followed. Straight for Mars the ship darted, with the speed of a meteor, but it could not shake off the circling bombs.

"Someone," said Svenga, "is pretty smart. What we have picked up for our trouble is five satellites, gentlemen. They swing in fixed orbits and it would be dangerous for us to *disturb* their equilibrium."

"Satellites?" cried Pavlovich. "That means that we can never land!"

Nicholas the First said nothing. To this there was no answer. Doomed to hurtle through empty void, with five explosive satellites. Soon a meteor would strike one of them, and it would be the end...

But to the Elder Race, neither such torture, nor such a chance for further damage could be countenanced. Instead, Nicholas the First and his ships were pursued toward the asteroid belt and there, among the tiny debris worlds, they sought to escape, but found that collision could not be avoided as the great rays of the Elders' ships drove them upon the jagged fragments.

Even when they sought to escape in lifeboats, their action was useless. There, among the debris of an exploded world, flashes of light announced the doom of Nicholas the First, and a few more fragments of debris took up their complicated orbits in the Belt of the Lost Orb.

ON EARTH, the dero ships hurtled upward out of their secret caves, losing no time in deploying and hurling all they had at the Elder God ships. Men on Earth, without the aid of television or telescopes, saw vast thunderbolts greater than those of Nature light the void of space beyond the atmosphere. And they saw the dero ships blast into atomic disintegration like bright novae, lighting the world in the dawn of a new era.

Other dero ships dove at Agarthi, ancient, supercharged dis-ray batteries shaving off tops of mountains as they neared their objective. But Agarthi's great field screens were up and the experienced operators there blazed back with their much heavier stationary armament. Many a dero ship blasted into nothingness under that concentrated defensive fire, but also many an Agarthian operator was busy throwing in defensive screens where others were overloaded and shorted out. In the meantime, the great flagship of the Elder Gods lay hidden in a huge valley of the Himalayas, holding its far superior fire in case help should be required.

The dero, seeing that open attack was futile, fell to a secondary means of offense. They decided to turn upon the helpless surface world cities. In fact, subterranean dis-ray operators blasted several European cities out of existence before the Elder Gods decided to enter the battle.

Deploying themselves almost instantaneously about the world, through the utilization of extra-dimensional portation unknown to Man, they blasted through all field barriers with paralysis beams. Then they systematically swept powerful death rays through the caverns, sparing only certain secret places where tero colonies still lived. It was a clean sweep on the deros. Their last ship was blasted, and their last man died... It was the first overthrow of Evil's tyranny over Earth since Paradise had been abandoned.

Only one dero escaped, unobserved by all in the excitement of Armageddon. One lone survivor, Kar, himself, sped toward Venus in an ancient ship of space, together with a number of surface slaves whom he handled through the ro mech...

The next day after the battle a free world awakened to the awareness that a new age had begun. The Russians offered to cease hostilities, and the Asiatics rested on their guns, demoralized. Joyous communications flew across the world. Great plans for positive peace and social reorganization sprang into men's minds, in spite of the disgruntled Quislings who would be forced to relinquish their power and authority over many a duped nation...

IN CHICAGO, Michael Kent was a guest at the presidential residence. He and the president, plus a dozen senators, several governors and congressmen and representatives of the press, were having breakfast.

The president grinned, self-consciously. "There seems to be so much to talk about that we're all scared to begin," he said.

But that broke the ice.

"Mr. President," the man from the Chicago Sun opened up, "what would be the attitude of this government if a supposedly benevolent dictator, that is, if this so-called King of the World, demanded that we should accept his rule?"

"I see," smiled the president, resignedly, "that the discussion of the ages begin..."

And so it did. While a great babble of voices ensued, Kent became lost in thought. Because Germain had contacted him.

Your work, Germain telepathed to him, *has only begun, Slim. During the coming year you will represent the King of the World in the United States. In a short time you are to be brought to Agarthi for full instructions. In the meantime, you may be interested to know that Lillian is with me.*

Thank God, thought Kent. That makes me alive again. God bless you both, Steve. You deserve happiness.

So do you, Slim. There is much ahead for all of us. Incidentally, remember Dr. Borg? Guess what... He's here in Agarthi! Came and confessed all his sins about a week ago. Said he wanted to devote himself to the study and advancement of Agarthian science.

No, Steve, retorted Kent, mentally. That's wrong. Why, the man is a fiend who must be destroyed along with the dero.

But you forget we have mental conditioning machines. Borg is a changed man. He's something of a genius, you know. Given a worthy purpose, he can go far.

Well, I still say he doesn't deserve it, insisted Kent.

I think we will one day be glad we forgave the old goat.

Anyway, say hello to Lil, thought Kent.

She's here beside me now, replied Germain. *She's beautiful, the way they've dressed her. Say, incidentally, I've got some further good news, Slim. I'm going to get a special break. The Elders, before they leave for home, are going to take me on board one of their ships and give me a surgical going over.*

What? thought Kent.

Yes. They say Borg's operation was too lavish, left me too supercharged for my own good. So they're going to tone me down a bit and replace the artificial harness I've got in my head with real flesh. I don't know how, but they promise to do it. Afterwards, I'll look a little more normal and can stop wearing this silly turban.

More power to you! commented Kent.

Lillian just threw a kiss to me that she says is intended for you. How do you like that, and I'm supposed, to telepath it... Hey! Remember that dimple she always used to have, the one that got lost? It's come back. And she's trying to distract my thoughts with it...

Several senators saw Kent grin into empty space. They did not know how incongruous it seemed to Kent to receive mentally two words that he had heard from the lips of an old friend since childhood.

They were: *Jumpin' catfish!*

THE END

If you've enjoyed this book, you will not want to miss these terrific titles…

ARMCHAIR SCI-FI & HORROR DOUBLE NOVELS, $12.95 each

ARMCHAIR SCIENCE FICTION & FANTASY CLASSICS, $12.95 each

If you've enjoyed this book, you will not want to miss these terrific titles…

ARMCHAIR SCI-FI & HORROR DOUBLE NOVELS, $12.95 each

D-71   **THE DEEP END** by Gregory Luce
TO WATCH BY NIGHT by Robert Moore Williams

D-72   **SWORDSMAN OF LOST TERRA** by Poul Anderson
PLANET OF GHOSTS by David V. Reed

D-73   **MOON OF BATTLE** by J. J. Allerton
THE MUTANT WEAPON by Murray Leinster

D-74   **OLD SPACEMEN NEVER DIE!** John Jakes
RETURN TO EARTH by Bryan Berry

D-75   **THE THING FROM UNDERNEATH** by Milton Lesser
OPERATION INTERSTELLAR by George O. Smith

D-76   **THE BURNING WORLD** by Algis Budrys
FOREVER IS TOO LONG by Chester S. Geier

D-77   **THE COSMIC JUNKMAN** by Rog Phillips
THE ULTIMATE WEAPON by John W. Campbell

D-78   **THE TIES OF EARTH** by James H. Schmitz
CUE FOR QUIET by Thomas L. Sherred

D-79   **SECRET OF THE MARTIANS** by Paul W. Fairman
THE VARIABLE MAN by Philip K. Dick

D-80   **THE GREEN GIRL** by Jack Williamson
THE ROBOT PERIL by Don Wilcox

ARMCHAIR SCIENCE FICTION CLASSICS, $12.95 each

C-25   **THE STAR KINGS**
by Edmond Hamilton

C-26   **NOT IN SOLITUDE**
by Kenneth Gantz

C-32   **PROMETHEUS II**
by S. J. Byrne

ARMCHAIR SCIENCE FICTION & HORROR GEMS SERIES, $12.95 each

G-7   **SCIENCE FICTION GEMS, Vol. Seven**
Jack Sharkey and others

G-8   **HORROR GEMS, Vol. Eight**
Seabury Quinn and others